THE *Great White* MAGE

RISE OF THE PHOENIX

VILANA MAY

PARTRIDGE

A Penguin Random House Company

To order additional copies of this book, contact
Toll Free 800 101 2657 (Singapore)
Toll Free 1 800 81 7340 (Malaysia)
orders.singapore@partridgepublishing.com

www.partridgepublishing.com/singapore

For Jacob
For love
For dreams

Chapter 1

DREAMS OF FIRE . . . AGAIN

T he flames devoured my body as a scream ripped from my throat in pure agony.

I dredged up every last iota of my depleting power to keep my friends away; I didn't want them to burn too. As the night sky filled with the sounds of my anguished cries and the large clouds of smoke billowing from the fire that engulfed my body, his beautiful face that was so clear to me filled with utter crippling horror . . .

I awoke and jerked upright, sending my covers flying to the other end of the bed. Utterly drenched in sweat, I slowly knuckled the sleep from my eyes too hard and saw stars. *What a stupid dream.* I stretched. You'd think that after years of having the same dream every damn night I'd be used to it. But apparently that wasn't so, seeing as I still reacted the same way I did the first time since I hit puberty at twelve.

I had a quick shower to clear all traces of swear from my body. The hot water felt good on my oddly cold skin. After that, I left my room and went downstairs for the welcoming smell of fresh toast coming from the kitchen.

"Morning, dear," said Adrienne Peterson, my beautiful young mom.

"Good morning, Mom," I said. I reached across and grabbed a piece of toast and scarfed it down, washing it down with a glass of milk. "That stupid dream won't go away," was my way of starting morning conversation. She gave me her famous disapproving expression. I just grinned back and scarfed down two more slices of toast. "This is good," I said as a peace offering.

She just replied "Uh huh" and smiled at me patronisingly. After all, toast was good as long as it wasn't burnt.

"You should be getting to school now." Adrienne jokingly brandished her ladle at me. "Your father left almost half an hour ago."

"It's fine, Mom." I went over to the sink to wash my glass. "I'll just take the bike."

She brandished her ladle at me again. "I'm still not sure that I approve of sixteen-year-olds riding motorbikes."

I just grinned at her cheekily. "You know you won't stop me." And that was when I noticed the time. "Oh! Gotta go!"

I went upstairs to grab my backpack then I flew down and waved goodbye before dashing out the door. I dumped my bag into the bike basket and got on, revving the engine. I put it in gear and slowly edged out of the driveway, pressing the automatic button on my small remote control for the gates to open and sped in the direction of the school.

I relished the feeling of the wind against my face and the tug of my long, dark, glossy hair. For some odd reason unknown to myself, I felt a sense of dark foreboding. Even though the sun was shining on me brightly like my own personal spotlight, anxiety filled my chest for a moment. Before I had a chance to think about it, my beloved

Settleburg High School loomed into sight, and chased my weird moment away.

When I entered the school gates, I saw the usual crowd that waited for me every day without fail. I bit back a mischievous grin and revved the engine, purposely riding into them, making them scatter in panic like ants.

I took my helmet off, shaking my hair out. My friends came over to meet me, wary looks on their faces. "What?" I asked, feigning ignorance.

They mock glared. "Are you trying to kill us?" My best friend, Remora scowled at me. I lifted an eyebrow.

"*What?*" I repeated in pretend shock. I kept my face straight and they bought it, much to my amusement.

"Geez, you need to get your eyes checked." Remora rolled her eyes at me. "You almost rode into all of us just now."

I decided to tease her. "How do you know I didn't do it on purpose?"

"Yeah, right." Mark Henderson waved my attempt away with a scoff. I grinned.

Mark was my kind-of, sort-of boyfriend. We never really got around to telling each other how we felt yet, but we were very close to each other. Everyone said it was pretty obvious what we were to each other.

Mark slung his arm around my shoulder, taking my bag for me. "You guys go ahead; I'll walk her to class." I felt a faint blush crawl up my cheeks and looked down, letting my heavy curtain of thick, long black hair hide my face.

Someone whistled and the group laughed, moving off. Remora shot me a '*this is it*' look and bounced off to join the others, her strawberry-blonde curls bouncing together. She laughed loudly.

I tried not to scowl at her retreat. *What a devious creature.* She must have said something to him while they were waiting for me.

"So," he started all too casually. "how are you today? No weird dreams to wake you up in time for school?"

His words immediately and effectively ruined my mood. "Painful dreams," I corrected. "That'll be the day," I mumbled as an aside. He laughed, seeming to find my sentence funny in a way I didn't see.

"Actually . . ." he said, drawing it out. My breath caught, and I felt so nervous, I had to pee. Erk, I was becoming crude.

He turned to me. I realised that we had walked into our favourite hideout in school. It was an old janitor's room that wasn't used anymore, and the school didn't know what to do with it. My friends and I had cleaned it up nicely and used it for whatever we wanted—by which I mean studying and chatting—so the school turned a blind eye. Plus, my dad was the principal. That helped.

Mark looked me in the eye, reached into his pocket, and pulled out a box. My breath caught again and my heartbeat sped up.

"Wendy." He looked at me seriously. "Wendy, let me be your Peter Pan."

There was a beat.

I laughed hysterically till tears ran down my face. "Oh . . . my . . . God," I choked out. "That—was the—stupidest line—I ever heard!!" I burst into a new round of laughter. He was laughing, too.

"Yes." I managed. He smiled at me in relief and—with his thumb gently—wiped the tears that were still on my face. Then he opened his small box, and I saw the most beautiful intricate necklace in the world. It was small and held a tiny crystal in the middle with swirls of silver metal twisting and curling around it. For a moment, the silver reminded me of the flashing eyes of the beautiful boy from my dream.

"Turn around," he said. I turned. He gently brushed my hair aside and placed it around my neck. In the moment his skin came in contact with mine, my mind flashed back.

*   *   *

When we were ten, I was playing in the playground and ran and fell on my face. When I tried to get up, no one would help me because everyone had recently seen a Japanese ghost show, and they moved away from me because of my black hair. Mark didn't seem to care and ran to me, piggybacking me all the way home. At that time, he was much smaller than I was.

*   *   *

Mark turned me back to face him. I cracked a smile. He enveloped me in a warm hug, and I grinned so wide, I was sincerely grateful that my face didn't split open.

"Um, we're gonna be late for class," I mumbled into his shirt, always one to ruin a moment. We walked together in companionable silence, holding hands. Of course, we were completely late, but there was always the privilege of being the principal's daughter. Even so, no teacher would ever begrudge us any time, because Mark and I were the best students in school. The day passed like any other uneventful school day with the glaring exception that I was officially an item with Mark.

"So," he said, "when are you gonna introduce me to your parents?"

I cringed internally. "Uh, they already know you," I offered. "We grew up together, remember?"

"Nice try," Mark retorted dryly. "I meant introduce me as your boyfriend."

Yikes! My stomach felt all jittery and jelly-like when he said the word *boyfriend*. My heart thumped loudly, and I sighed.

"Okay, okay!" I groaned, feeling like I lost the fight before it even started. "You win again." I never really could win any arguments against him. Mark just smiled, as if it was a sure thing, which it was. After the final school bell rang, and we said goodbye to our friends, I gave Mark my extra helmet.

He sat behind me on my bike, and I rode us to my home. He started to look nervous. I was secretly pleased to see him nervous about meeting my parents. At least it meant that I wasn't the only one who was nervous. We walked into my house hand in hand and I was surprised to see my parents already sitting down on the "discussion sofa" and waiting for me. They seemed to be equally surprised by my coming in holding hands with Mark.

"Hi, Mom. Hi, Dad." I said amiably. "Err, there's something I have to tell you . . ." I really didn't know how to continue. It's not like I had ever done this before. They seemed to know already, but they looked a bit uncomfortable somehow. *Hmmm, wonder why that is?*

I bit my lip and wracked my brain desperately for a way to say what I needed to say. After I opened and closed my mouth several times with no results, Mark took over and told them that we were together. I was relieved to see my parents accept it so easily.

"There is something I have to tell you too," my dad said. I saw an odd look on my mom's face and started to feel kind of queasy. Mark and I exchanged a "the fark?" look.

My dad looked me in the eye. *Uh, oh. That was always bad.* I tried not to squirm under his gaze. "Yes, Dad? Would you like to get on with it?" I said, breaking the awkward silence. My heartbeat picked up as I knew by intuition that he was about to deliver bad news.

"We're moving." He exhaled the words in a rush.

"Excuse me?" I asked, clearly not hearing right.

Mark had turned to stone beside me.

"We are moving." Alex repeated. "I had an offer to be the principal in a smaller town, and your mom would be delighted with the change. I myself would rather settle down somewhere quiet—"

"No!" I exploded, shocking everyone, myself included. My father just looked at me. I hated that look. That was the look that told me no matter what happened, I had no say in it. "But, Dad, I just . . . my friends, and Mark," I sputtered nonsensical babble. He just kept a level look, and I knew any argument I made would be in vain.

I grabbed Mark's hand, and we left my house like the devil himself was after us.

We went to Mark's house two blocks away, and when we reached his front gate, he grabbed me and kissed me hard, feverishly, like he never wanted to let me go. My entire body zinged with electricity and heat. He pulled back with a strangely resigned look on his face. The expression didn't belong in the heat of this passionate moment. My first-kiss euphoria died away, and it was replaced by a desperate feeling.

"What?" I asked. He straightened his back and looked straight ahead, the expression on his face now unreadable. This look filled me with worry. "*What?*" I repeated adamantly. He sighed and thawed, looking at me ruefully.

"You just became my girlfriend today and now I'm going to lose you," he said, sadness creeping into his voice and pinching my heart. I hugged him fiercely.

"Never," I swore grimly. "you will never lose me." I felt his chest shake with laughter.

"We're getting a little melodramatic, don't you think?" He hugged me back. "Well, at least it's a month from now. Are you okay with long-distance relationships?" he wondered wistfully.

I pulled back and shrugged. "How would I know? I've never been in a relationship before." I reminded him. And then I sighed. "I'm going to miss everyone so much."

He smiled sadly. I turned, and walked back to my house, glaring at my parents, maintaining the stony silent treatment, and slamming all the doors in my way to my room. I threw myself onto my bed. Why? Everything was just coming together! Why did this have to happen now? Screw that, why did this have to happen at all? I was just nominated cheer captain, I had the top grades, I was everybody's role model and I was at the peak! I had the most wanted guy at school as my boyfriend and now everything was ruined. I passionately cried myself to sleep that night.

For the next month I was the pinnacle of busy. I was busy giving all my choreography for the cheer squad, I was busy dating Mark as much as I could, I was busy keeping my grades prefect, I was busy spending all my time with my friends. Most of all, I was busy packing my things.

We were taking most of our furniture, but had to leave some things behind. I secretly kissed these things, leaving a part of me behind with them. We were apparently staying in a three-storey bungalow without the automatic workings. I decided to hate the house from the start even before seeing it. I didn't want to see it — ever — if possible.

On the eve of my separation with real life, my friends threw me a humongous farewell party. It was even better than last year's prom. Even my dad had a farewell party at one of the minister's house down the street. Everyone loved my dad. Alex was one of those charismatic people that everyone easily adored instantly. I inherited that charismatic part of him, I guess, the proof being the huge crowd crying, saying they would miss me even though I was sure I'd never seen most of them before.

Did Remora invite the whole school? I wondered fondly. It was just like her to do that. I suppressed the tears that were threatening to flow. I was really going to miss this city. The new buildings, the modern-ness of a city was cool and homey and I didn't want to leave, ever.

The next day was a Saturday, so everyone was free to see us off as we left in our car. I waved until I couldn't see anyone anymore. I glared out the window though I didn't see anything, and focused on the ear-splitting heavy metal music that seemed bent on damaging my eardrums. I'd gotten a new pair of earphones just for that.

My plan to hate the bungalow failed miserably. It was amazing, like something out of a fairy tale. The roof was red tiled and there was ivy creeping along the walls. It wasn't the messy kind of ivy, more like the decorative ivy, the kind where you'd expect Romeo to suddenly appear and climb up to throw pebbles at the beautiful French floor length windows. Wow.

The front gate was further from the driveway compared to our old house. There was a small grassy path that split off from the driveway into the garden. We now had a huge front lawn, side gardens and a cool backyard that had a swimming pool with a fountain on the side and a drinks bar under a cove. I couldn't hate it at all.

I went into the house. Major wow, again. The rest of the house was even more impressive than the outside. I looked into all the doors and found a cute room with a window seat, a chestnut wardrobe, and a king-sized four-poster bed, and immediately booked the room as mine. My parents laughed at my stubborn expression, like the thought of them saying "no" never crossed their mind.

Yeah, right.

There was a one-week holiday in this interesting town called Queenstown. Maybe they used to have a monarchy that was ruled by the matriarch. In any case, I had no desire to see the rest of the town, preferring to lock myself in my room and IM my friends and talk on the phone all day with my too-far boyfriend. At least they still treated me the same way, but after a long time, would they start to forget me? I bitterly cried myself to sleep that night as well.

Just like all my nights, the same dream haunted me.

* * *

"Tie 'er up!" someone yelled in a heavy accent. "Make sure the witch doesn't get away!"

I struggled, wanting so badly to use my powers to free myself, but if I did, the people would have their suspicions confirmed, and they would hunt down my dearest friends too. I felt my friends' presence; they were running with their awesome magic speed to come and save me. No! I must not allow them to come. Before I could do anything, the humans were pouring oil over me and torches of fire were flung at me. The pain was overwhelming. My magic instantly went to the body parts of me that were burning and healed, only to be burned again.

As my magic reserves depleted, I remembered my friends' presence and summoned all my remaining power to create a field that kept them away. But my magic was running out, so the perimeter wasn't as wide as I wanted it to be, and I saw him. He was the most beautiful boy in the world. Just seeing his face almost made me change my mind and kill all the people around me so that we could live in peace. Almost. The flames grew and the pain intensified tenfold.

I focused all my concentration on keeping my pain inside so that he wouldn't be so scared, but the gruesome smell of burning flesh alerted my senses, and the pain that had built up in my body shoved up my throat in painful rough bubbles, and an incredibly bloodcurdling scream exploded out of me. His eyes were riveted on mine and they were filled with agony.

And somehow, I knew my time was up. Before I closed my eyes for the last time, I gave him the sweetest smile I could manage. Let him remember me as the most powerful witch that gave up her life for the humans . . .

*   *   *

I woke up with a violent jerk, gasping for air like a fish out of water and sweating like you wouldn't believe. My dream was never so intense before. I wondered what had changed. The boy's face was clearer now, and he was breathtakingly beautiful. Everything about him was light, like an angel. My dream had never left me so shaken before. It seems that my dream was growing, too.

I groaned, suddenly remembering where I was. Then I groaned again, remembering what day it was. It was Monday, a school day, and the holidays were over.

Chapter 2

NEW AND REALLY HATING IT

I stomped loudly on the way down the stairs, I stomped loudly on the way to the car, and I stomped loudly from the car to the school. Alex — my dear father — gripped my arm and pulled me back.

"What?" I ground out. There were so many reasons for me to be a grouch today, and I had never been a patient girl.

"Wendy, please. You know I did this for all of us —"

"Whatever." I cut him off harshly.

"Okay, then. I promise you that you will like the school here." He surrendered and gave me a hopeful smile which I ungracefully forced myself to return. Then I slumped away in the direction of the school registration while Alex headed in the direction of the office.

There were students everywhere. Some were leaning against walls and talking, some were the usual jocks playing around, some were cheerleaders doing morning practice, and then there were Goth kids in pretty cool outfits, and the nerdy kids with glasses and thick books. I watched in distaste as a dorky looking boy was pushed around by a group of jocks.

I sighed and walked onwards. My glossy black hair was flowing past my waist and it helped to cover up that I was dressed city-style. The town-style was much . . . less-style.

As I walked by, I drew attention from everyone. And I meant everyone; the jocks stopped roughhousing, the cheerleaders stopped cheering, the dorks looked away from their books and the Goths . . . stared.

I suppressed a shudder from the creepiness of it and continued walking towards the registration office on the other side of the school like this occurred every day. Well, it did occur every day, even back home. Just not so intensely.

I entered the creaky office and shuddered, going straight to the counter. I smiled fakely at the pale old lady sitting there. Something about her just pissed me off, and I knew it had everything to do with my mood, and nothing to do with her. "Hello, there. I'm new here, can I get the schedule?"

"Why, yes, of course." The old lady seemed to smile as fakely as I did. She searched around for a while and handed me my schedule. "Are you the new principal's daughter?"

"That's right." I gave her the creepiest smile I could come up with to hopefully creep her off my back. It worked magnificently. She returned a rather weak smile and waved me off.

I looked at the paper. First class: English. Yay. My favourite. Note the sarcasm. I decided then and there that I was going to make life hell for all those who were unfortunate enough to cross my path. It was payback time. And for all those who knew me, I was the worst thing that could happen to someone if I was in a bad mood.

Leaving the office, I felt an odd wave of vertigo, as if I'd been lying down for too long and got up too suddenly. I looked around, wondering what the cause of it was, but there was no one around.

There was no one around.

I shivered; feeling like those words were as false as the old lady's smile. It felt like there were one too many eyes on my back for my liking. I took two deep, cleansing breaths, and started in the direction of block C, where the map said my English class was. Again, I felt like there were many eyes on me, monitoring my every movement. I quickened my pace, hoping to stop feeling that way, suddenly too creeped out to care about how I looked to others; the new girl walking way too fast to get to class.

"Excuse me?"

I jumped violently right out of my skin and gave a little shriek. My heart seemed to have jumped into my throat and pumped there. I turned to my left, where the voice came from and saw this tiny girl about a head shorter than me. She had long white-blonde hair that flowed past her butt. Her eyes were an enchanting deep blue framed with thick dark lashes and her features looked rather chiselled. And she also just popped out of nowhere.

I'd never seen anybody like her, yet I felt as if I should know her somewhere deep down in my heart. She looked like a doll God would have made. Impulsively, I smiled at her pleasantly, completely forgetting my oath to myself that I would destroy everyone's lives.

"Yeah? What?" My words reminded me of my terrible oath, and I slipped back into my malicious mood. "I can't help you out, because I'm new," I said snidely, feeling like a witch with a capital B.

She smiled at me serenely. It annoyed me to the core.

"I'm not asking for help. I'm giving it," She informed me. "I was assigned to be your guide."

I thought about it. "Just point me in the right direction. I don't need a guide."

She smiled at me knowingly. Then she turned around, and walked straight down the hallway. I followed after her

14

since it was the obvious thing to do. I realised that the way she said "guide" sounded much . . . more. Like there was some weird hidden meaning behind it. I shook my head, trying to physically throw my weird thoughts out of it.

"May I know your name?" She asked. I walked next to her and contemplated keeping my mouth shut. Then I sighed, realising how childish I was being.

"Wendy Fletcher. And you are?"

"I am Snowy Boyle," she said with a smile. "I am sixteen like you. I was chosen as your guide because we had the most classes together."

I nodded. I didn't ask for her explanation but I was glad she told me. I would have thought of that much later and creeped myself out. We passed a few classes and the students were all very quiet. As we passed, their eyes latched onto me until I was out of sight. I unsuccessfully tried to suppress a shudder.

"It's because we rarely ever have new students from out of town," Snowy explained when she saw me shiver. "I'd say you're the first in around seven years or so."

"Great," I said unenthusiastically. As my mood plummeted, the lights above us started flickering. I hated flickering lights. It was always too creepy for me. Snowy looked at me and I could have sworn I saw a weird emotion pass across her face, but it disappeared so quickly I wasn't sure that I hadn't imagined it. Then she smiled at me and I chilled a bit, noticing that the lights had also stopped flickering.

"Does that light thing happen often? Because I really can't stand it. Even when I'm watching horror movies, the flickering lights part is always the only part I can't stand. Bleeding people with guts pouring out can't compare." I realised I was crapping and clamped my mouth shut. I bit my lip and groaned internally. It took me forever to break the habit of biting my lips.

Snowy looked at me and for the first time I saw that she thought there was something wrong with me. There was a look on her face that said "I can't believe you just said that". Naturally, I went on the defensive.

"What? Can't a girl have some irrational fears?" I grumbled. A smile returned to her face and she nodded.

"I wouldn't call that irrational though," Snowy said. At least, that's what I thought she said, but I couldn't be sure. She said that line too softly. And then she finally turned to face a classroom. Finally! I was starting to consider dropping out of school what with the amount of staring. Huh, home-schooling didn't seem like a bad idea.

I wondered if there was something on my hair to make them stare so much. I looked down at myself to confirm that I was wearing pants. Yupp, jeans there alright.

"Sorry we're late; I was leading the new student in." I heard Snowy's voice say. Instantly, the classroom chatter dried up into complete silence. I groaned internally. If they kept this up, Alex or no Alex I was gonna slug somebody. The last thought pulled me up short.

Whoa, I thought to myself. *Hold your horses, girl. Since when were you such a violent person?*

"Fletcher?" Snowy's voice called. I realised that I was standing paralysed outside the door and took a deep breath. It was now or never. I tried not thinking about how much I would prefer never. It just took three steps to go into the class.

I took the three steps in quick bursts before I could talk myself out of it. I automatically looked around and then wished I hadn't. Snowy stood at the front of the class with the teacher at his desk. The classroom itself was fairly normal, though the students were anything but.

All eyes in the classroom latched onto my face and hung on. I finally succeeded in suppressing a shiver and quickly looked down.

"Wendy Fletcher?" boomed the teacher's voice. My eyes went up to look at the teacher.

He was a moderately tall guy with balding grey hair and had washed out brown eyes. He also had a beer belly, and quite a big one, too. He wore light brown slack pants and a matching white khaki shirt.

"Well, are you Wendy Fletcher?" he boomed again, and this time, there was a hint of impatience in his voice. I realised that I'd forgotten to answer him because I'd been busy checking him out. Before I could hope that no one saw me check out a teacher, I remembered that I was an eye magnet today, so no hope.

"Yeah, unless you were expecting someone else," I replied nonchalantly. You see, the key to getting teachers to like you was not just being polite. It was treating them as equals, but also letting them know you respected them. In this case, I wasn't interested in getting the teacher to like me, so I threw respect out the window.

I felt a small twinge of guilt because teachers deserved respect. Also, this would probably reflect badly on Alex. However, my bad mood was a lot fouler than my guilt, so I didn't apologize.

"No, we weren't expecting someone else," he said flatly. Yikes. I was tempted to reply with "Then why'd you ask?" but I knew that would be pushing it, so I kept my mouth shut.

"You will sit beside Miss Boyle today until we can work out new seating arrangements," he said. "Now, would you like to introduce yourself to your classmates?"

I was sincerely tempted to say no, but the expression on his face left no doubt in my mind that I didn't really have a choice in the matter. Someone chuckled softly and the sound helped me relax a bit. So they *can* make sounds in my presence.

I turned slowly to face them. Snowy walked past me and went to a seat in the middle row, three columns from the right. There was an empty chair beside her. I tried looking at their faces and was further relieved to know that they actually had expressions. Thank heavens for that. However, most of them just looked amused. Great, first day in school and I was already the class clown.

"I'm Wendy Elise Fletcher. I'm from Settleburg City," I said dully, like I changed schools every day. Everyone stared back at me, an expectant look on their faces. Some even looked excited to see a city kid. I wondered if I should be saying something more.

I instinctively looked at Snowy and she smiled encouragingly. Yupp, I'm definitely supposed to say something more. Since I had no idea what to say, I kept my mouth shut and waited for someone to nudge me in the right direction.

"Is that all, Miss Fletcher?" The teacher asked in his booming voice. Seriously, his voice was like a boom box. I could feel vibrations in my chest when he spoke. Well, even the teacher wasn't going to give me any hints, so I shrugged.

"I guess," was my brilliant reply. This time, there was more than one someone who chuckled at my expense. I somehow managed to keep a scowl off my face. I wasn't sure if it was a good idea to pass myself off as a bad person, despite my earlier fury.

"Alright, then. Go to your seat." He sighed. It sounded more like rumbling thunder than a sigh though. "I am Mr Kennedy, your homeroom and English teacher."

I noticed that all of them looked a little bit disheartened and I wondered again what I was supposed to say that I wasn't saying. Snowy's look of encouragement had deflated and she wore a tight smile. I suppressed another sigh. It would seem I was suppressing one too many sighs today. That was probably bad for health; suppressed emotion, and all.

I realised I was crapping even in my own head and tried to blank out all my thoughts. I let my bag slip down my shoulder to land on the floor beside my desk. Luckily, Mr Kennedy started speaking, so I had something to concentrate on.

"All of you know what book we will be doing for our English class this semester, however, I will say it again for Miss Fletcher, and for those that I know have already forgotten." He boomed. He went behind his desk to the whiteboard and picked up a blue whiteboard marker. "The book this time is *Cinderella*."

I was surprised. Wasn't *Cinderella* a bedtime fairy tale? I was actually expecting us to do one of Shakespeare's plays. I actually went through *The Twelfth Night* in my previous school. Last year, we did *The Tempest*.

"I want all of you to write three essays by the end of this semester. The first is due on the first of next month, which is in two weeks." Mr Kennedy continued, interrupting my mental ranting. "Each essay will make up twenty per cent of the overall grade for this semester."

There was a collective groan throughout the class, and I was relieved. They were normal kids. I'd actually started to think of the kids in the school as zombies. Before more nonsense could punctuate my thoughts, Mr Kennedy spoke again.

"I want you to write the first essay on the characters. Write an elaborate character sketch and what you think of them," he instructed. I noticed that he wrote "*Cinderella*, 3 essays, 20%, 1=character study" on the board. I heard a rustle of paper and looked around. A few of them were taking notes. I considered taking down the notes, but that would mean I had to reach into my bag to pull out my stationery, and I seriously just didn't want to call attention to myself. Plus, the notes were cake for someone like me. Gosh, that sounded so conceited.

Meanwhile, Mr Kennedy had busied himself by walking over to a book closet at the front right corner of the room. He took out a key that was hanging on a chain around his neck and proceeded to unlock the closet.

Wow, either there was something seriously valuable in there or he was a seriously forgetful person and was afraid to misplace the keys. I couldn't imagine why else one would feel the need to keep a book closet key on a chain around one's neck.

While I continued creating world-class nonsense in my head, Mr Kennedy had reached into the closet and hefted a pile of moderately slim books. I mean, I supposed they were moderately slim. To me, they were tiny, only half an inch thick. I had an entire personal library of fictional books in my possession, most of which were at the very least two inches thick.

Then he put the books on one of the front students' table and asked him to pass it along with only one simple instruction, and a glare in my direction. "Read it."

Chapter 3

OLD FRIENDS AND NEW FREAKS

After English, it was Math, and all I could say about it was that I didn't want to say anything about it. I was incredibly grateful that Snowy had been present. *Let's not think about the alternative*, I thought to myself. *While on that subject, let's not think about Math at all.*

I sighed out loud this time. I was tired of suppressing sighs since it probably wasn't very healthy. Snowy elbowed me good naturedly and smiled, rolling her eyes.

"It wasn't that bad, you know."

"I beg to differ," I moaned heavily and gave a short laugh. I couldn't do much beside that, since the entire cafeteria insisted on staring me down in utter silence. Snowy caught on and stopped trying to cheer me up, allowing me to wallow in my misery.

It probably didn't matter what I did anymore. They probably all thought I was the craziest thing to ever grace this blue green rock. Yes, I meant the Earth. I frowned slightly. I was starting to sound crazy, even to myself. I didn't have to wonder why, though.

I was smart and I figured out early on that I was crapping a lot in my head to fill the outside silence that felt almost physical. The line moved again and we moved forward. There was the scraping sound of the lunch lady scooping up whatever food there was and dumping it on some kid's plate. Yeah, the cafeteria was *that* silent.

Snowy was standing beside me instead of in front of me because she figured I needed the support. She figured right, of course. In fact, she seemed to be so attuned to my feelings and moods that it was hard believe we've never met before. More than that, we should have been damn close for her to know me so well.

Maybe that's because she does *know you.*

I sighed again and waved that thought away. This was the first time we've ever met, for heaven's sake. Maybe she was an empath, someone who could easily read the feelings of those around them, not just me. The line moved again and we moved along.

"What are you having?" Snowy asked to fill the tense silence. I looked over at the food selection, and my already minimal appetite evaporated.

"Just . . . juice," I said weakly, noticing some boxed drinks. The drinks were thankfully not homemade; they were a brand that I recognized from my city, so I deemed them reliable.

"Are you sure you can survive on just juice?" she frowned, looking a bit concerned. "I can barely survive on a three course meal."

That sounded insane. "What?" I croaked.

She laughed. "Oh, don't worry, that's just me. I'm a food maniac. I have a high rate of metabolism, so I can afford it."

"Ah, I see," I replied.

There was a beat of silence. The line moved again and we walked forward.

"How much exactly do you eat per day?" I couldn't resist asking.

"Hmmm, let's see. I have bacon, ham, toast, eggs, cereal and milk for breakfast every day. Then I have brunch, but that changes from day to day. Then I have lunch, followed by tea-time which usually consists of finger sandwiches, tea cakes, scones and, well, tea. Then I have dinner and after that, supper." She listed them off on her fingers.

My jaw had fallen a bit for every meal she listed out and now I snapped it shut. "Where does it all go?" I exclaimed. I noticed that the kids had started to look away and talk amongst themselves, so my exclamation didn't echo too loudly. As it was, more than a few heads turned my way again.

I ducked my head.

Snowy had a misty look in her eyes. To my surprise, I actually saw tears shimmering there.

"What did I say?" I panicked. She shook her head and laughed quietly, blinking the tears away.

The line moved and we took two steps forward.

"It's just that you used to . . . I mean, I used to have a friend who was so much like you. She always said the same thing to me. 'Where does it all go, Gwenwyn?'" Snowy smiled wistfully, and then she blinked, her eyes wide, her hand flying to her mouth as if she just said something wrong. "I meant 'Snowy'."

"Oh . . . I see." Then I had no idea what to say. I wanted to ask what happened to her friend but I was worried that it would be insensitive. Did her friend die? Move away like I moved away from my home?

The thought made my chest ache for the life I'd left behind. I thought about Mark and wondered if he was thinking about me as well. Was Remora having parties with a new best friend, or was she feeling lonely without me? I hoped she found a nice person to be best friends with.

The line moved again and we moved along in silence. This silence thing was getting really old, really fast. Suddenly, I remembered that Snowy had said "Gwenwyn".

"Who's Gwenwyn?" I asked her. She looked to the left, and I wondered if she was looking for someone, or hiding her face from me.

"We—my friend and I—that is, always used to play medieval games and such. My name was Gwenwyn," She said with a touch of sadness.

"Sorry," I said, because it somehow felt like I was responsible for putting the sadness there.

She just shrugged. The line moved and we were finally in front of the lunch lady. I let Snowy order first, because she was supposed to be in front of me.

I noticed that Snowy's pile was as high as a mountain.

"Next," called the lunch lady's bored voice. She sounded raspy, like there was sandpaper in her throat.

I pointed to one of the boxed drinks. "Peach tea, please."

"Just that?" she rasped. When I nodded, she squinted at me. "You sure that will last you, girl?"

"Yeah," I squeaked. She was kinda creepy. There were two hairy warts on her nose. I saw genuine concern in her eyes, though, so I was ashamed of myself.

"One fifty," she said, turning around to pluck the boxed drink off the shelf.

I put two bucks on the counter and as she was giving me my change, I gave her a bit of advice.

"Do you have a sore throat?" I asked sympathetically. She blinked at me and nodded.

"Why, yes, I do. Just started feeling it yesterday," she grumbled.

"Did it itch at the back of your mouth first or deeper down your throat first?" I asked.

"Hmmm." She looked at me, trying to figure out if I was playing a trick on her. When she saw my sincerity, she sighed. "Deep down my throat here," she said, and pointed to the base of her throat, just above the hollow of her neck.

"Then you should slice a lemon very thinly and soak it overnight in pure honey, don't mix it with water. Then eat two slices after every meal. The skin won't be bitter anymore, so you should eat the skin, too; it's very nourishing." She looked surprised at my words, and then she placed my change on the counter, took out a notepad and wrote it down, which shocked me in turn.

"Is that it?" she asked eagerly. *Wow, am I a celebrity chef?*

"Well, you can eat the slices but don't drink the honey," I said, feeling awkward.

"Why not?" she rasped, puzzled. Snowy looked at me, and there was the strange look on her face that disappeared again quickly. The entire school seemed to lean in, hanging on to every word I said.

"Well, think of the honey as a provider. It gives the lemon its nutrients and takes away the lemon's bad ones," I explained. I quickly picked up my change to end the weird conversation. "Thanks."

Snowy led me away from the food line and went outside. I was confused because there were quite a few spaces to sit. But when I saw where she took me, I didn't complain.

There was a mini garden with pink, purple and yellow flowers everywhere. In the centre, there was a small fountain and there were four benches facing the fountain, arranged in a square. And a tall girl with shoulder length blonde hair that was surprisingly stylish was chatting to two other girls. The other two girls had light brown hair, one closer to blonde than the other. They were all wearing cheerleader outfits.

"Excuse me," said Snowy quietly, but she might as well have roared it out. The three cheerleaders turned their heads, saw us, and paled. They looked afraid — no — terrified.

"Oh . . . Snowy Boyle," said the blonde. Her voice shook a little when she said her name. "I just wanted to talk to your . . . friend," She said, indicating me by inclining her head.

"Say it fast." Snowy's voice was scary. It sounded quiet but deadly. I felt a light breeze charged with energy.

"You . . . Would you like to join our squad? Try outs are this Wednesday, bring your own audio CD and an original routine." She speed-talked, making her words run into each other. She seemed surprised at her own antics and shivered, looking at Snowy with fear.

What was up with that?

"My name is Wendy Fletcher," I said, not liking that she referred to me as "you". "I will think about it, but don't regret it if I come. I'm a squad captain." My tone left no doubt that if I join; I would take over the captain's spot.

"Leave," said Snowy. "This is no place for you. If I ever see anyone come here again . . ." She smiled, and I paled before remembering she wasn't talking to me. That smile belonged on a calm serial killer. "Pass that along, will you?"

The girls nodded and more or less fled the garden.

"Well," I started. "Well, that was . . . Hey, do you own the school or something? Or are you a royal?"

Snowy chuckled. "You could say that my family is one of the founding families of this school."

"*One* of them? How many founding families are there?" I wondered aloud. I managed to push the incident out of my mind. I could do that sort of thing. If I didn't like it, it didn't happen. I plucked the straw from the side of the box and tried to push it out of the plastic wrap.

"Five." A guy's voice said right at my left ear, at the same time a hand took the straw from behind me. I jumped violently, the juice box flying out of my hands. A tall girl with flowing fire-red locks of hair plucked the flying box neatly out of the air. She wore a simple white dress that came down to her knees. Nice purple ballet flats covered her feet.

A guy came around my bench and gave my straw to me—without the plastic wrap. He was dark haired, a dark brown that I'd never seen in anyone's hair before, with a pale blue stripe cutting across his fringe. He grinned at me, revealing nice, strong white teeth. And his startling blue eyes twinkled at me, somehow so familiar, yet not. His eyes were almost the same shade as Snowy's.

I took the straw mechanically. "Thanks," I croaked, my heart still beating fast from shock. The girl came over to me as well and handed me my drink.

Snowy was smiling softly.

"So, who are you guys?" I tried for nonchalance and barely succeeded. The guy chuckled and I distracted myself by poking the straw into the aluminium hole.

"They are . . . your friends." I looked up to see Snowy smiling at me.

"Right, yeah, okay. Hello, friends." I let my voice drown with sarcasm. The guy and the girl sat on the bench opposite of me and Snowy sat on the one on my right. If you ever wanted to see complete happiness, then you should have been there. There was pure happy contentedness on their faces, as if I completed them. It creeped me out, at the same time, made *me* feel complete.

Great, Fletcher, throw in with the freaks.

"I mean, what are your names?" I sighed. They didn't seem to want to move from their comfy spots, so I had to ask again. The moment was broken and their faces looked a bit strained. They looked at each other, giving the *not yet* look. Not yet for what? Telling me their names?

"I am Jason McIntyre," said the guy. He smiled and ran a hand through his hair, making the blue stripe sparkle. "You can call me Jase. I am the son of . . . well, it's not important."

His parents weren't important? What was he going to introduce his parents for, anyway? Oh! Was that the extra thing that I was supposed to say but didn't?

"I am Summer Herrington," said the girl. I nodded. The name was very apt. Very . . . red. "Daughter of . . ." she blinked and stopped as well, biting her lips. Ooookay. I watched as Summer elbowed Jason in the ribs playfully when he grinned at her conspiratorially, and wondered if they were dating.

"So . . . I'm supposed to introduce my parents?" I rolled my eyes at the weirdness of it all. "I'm Wendy Fletcher, daughter of Alex Fletcher and Adrienne Peterson." I cracked a small smile, feeling like it was in the medieval times where they announced their name and everything they owned with it. Pffft.

"Welcome, then, Wendy Fletcher." They smiled. All three of them. I nodded to indulge them and sucked on my drink. Snowy really could eat a lot. There was a mountain on her plate. Really, I was sure I could measure the height of the pile of food in inches.

They started asking me basic, simple questions and the weirdness seemed to pass. Well, either that or I'd gotten used to it. Erk.

Jase was in the middle of asking me what my favourite book was when my phone rang. It was a special caller ringtone, set only for Mark's number. The song was "She Will Be Loved" by Maroon 5. I know, old, but lovable.

The excitement flew through my whole body, and I scooped my phone out of my pocket faster than you could say "yikes".

"Hello?" I breathed true life for the first time of the day.

"Hey, babe!" Mark's enthusiastic voice came through the speakers loud and clear. "How's it going over there? Survive-able?"

I laughed. "Oh, please, you know I can survive anything." I caught the three of them exchanging a look, but I ignored it. "I just really, really miss you." My voice broke on the last word. There was a silence at the other end of the line. Heaviness filled my chest.

"I know, babe, I miss you, too. I feel like I've been going crazy not seeing you. The longest we ever separated was like, a few hours, and that was so we could sleep." He sighed heavily. "I feel like a part of me is missing without you."

I bit my lip as tears stung the back of my eyes. "Same here. Well, I have three new friends!" I changed the subject before I could become a complete mess and contribute to the water fountain.

"Really? Only three? What's going on?" he demanded and there was concern on the edge of his voice.

"Erm . . ."

"Wendy, please."

"It's the kids here. They stare. They don't do anything but stare and it's freaking me out," I told him passionately. There was a cough from one of the three 'friends' and I amended. "Most of them."

There was a small cuss. "Wendy, I'll try to convince your dad to let you stay here. We can make it a long term sleepover at my place, or Remora's place. She didn't want me to tell you, but she hasn't been sleeping well since you left," Mark said, and I knew he was desperately grasping at straws.

"You can try," I said dubiously. Then the end-of-break time bell rang and I sighed. "That's the bell. I'll catch up with you later. I love you."

"I love you, too. So much." He sounded choked.

I wanted to say goodbye but it wouldn't come. Then the line went dead. I was surprised. Did Mark hang up on me? I checked the phone and realised that there was no line. I groaned loudly.

Well, at least no one had to hang up.

Chapter 4

CURIOUSER AND CURIOUSER

I'd say the highlight of the day was my last class before going home from school. I wondered if the staring and the silence would ever stop. I remembered that they had talked in the cafeteria. I perked up at that thought, but then I recalled that as soon as I spoke, they all paid attention again, and my spirits sank to my knees.

I was in the last class of the day, World History, the only class I had without Snowy. I noticed that there was one empty seat in the class, and wondered who was absent. Then I realised I wouldn't know anyway. Somehow, the mood in that class was a lot more different than the mood in the previous classes.

Everyone seemed a lot less . . . tense and silent. There was the usual class chatter that always ensued whenever there wasn't a teacher. Some of them even smiled at me, and I smiled back. Now, this felt like what it would have been if I'd gone to a normal school.

The person beside me, a boy with smooth black hair that came down to his shoulders and a bad boy grin introduced himself to me.

"Hey, what's up?" He said. I shrugged, unable to speak from surprise that someone was actually talking to me. "I'm Michael Simons. Son of Jonah Simons and Danielle Roman." He offered me his hand to shake.

"Wendy Fletcher, daughter of Alex Fletcher and Adrienne Peterson." I shook his hand. "Why is everyone suddenly normal?" I couldn't stop myself from asking. Well, aside from the fact that they announced who their parents were. That was not normal.

Michael turned his head and his pale blue eyes pierced into mine. He put his cheek on one hand and sighed. "It's not you that's the problem. It's the Blood."

"The Blood?" I was mystified.

"Yeah." Michael nodded. "The Blood are what we call the founding families. We have to treat them with respect." I could hear the disgust in his voice. "Actually, it's more than the school. It's the whole town. The Blood are the founders of the whole town."

"Oh, I see," I said. That explained a lot. Why no one spoke in Snowy's presence. It wasn't me at all. That made me wonder if being friends with Snowy would hold me back from enjoying a normal school life.

"Well, they seem to be interested in you, so I'm not sure whether I should be treating you respectfully." Michael continued. He had a weighted look in his eyes. "They only ever speak to those they deem equal to them." He snorted and rolled his eyes.

I blinked. "Well, respect as a person, yes. But the whole silence thing is seriously annoying and creepy."

He smiled genuinely and his light blue eyes sparkled. I have a boyfriend, yes, but I couldn't ignore incredible hotness when it's staring me in the face.

"Erm, also, Snowy's only guiding me because we have the most classes together," I said quickly to distract myself.

He shook his head. "That's not a coincidence. Do you wanna hear my theory?" he leaned in closer to me and I found that I had hard time breathing. This dude oozes 'guy' pheromones like you wouldn't believe. I tore my eyes away from his impressive biceps.

"Sure!" I leaned away from him, but he motioned me closer, his expression telling me that he had to say it softly.

"I think they know you. They wanted you to come, so they invited your dad." He looked around and saw the two kids in front of us looking, so he levelled a cool gaze at them. They turned around quickly and pretended to be busy with other stuff.

"They can easily arrange that sort of thing. And schedules, too, no problem." He lowered his voice. "So I think you have the Blood, too, you just don't know it."

I stared at him. "Uh . . . I don't think so." Okay, maybe this place was crazy after all. "I was born and raised in Settleburg City. I think it's totally been that way for generations." I said, remembering all my ancestor's graves in the Settleburg Cemetery.

"Really?" Michael frowned. For a really good looking bad-boy type, he seemed a bit too nerdy. Then he shrugged, turning back to the bad boy I thought he was. "Well, no matter, I don't give a damn."

He put his head on the table and started sleeping. I sighed. Well, that went well. Note the sarcasm.

A girl with generic brown hair who sat in front of me turned around with a smile on her face. "Hi, I'm Janet Watson."

"You don't have to introduce your parents," I said quickly. "I'm Wendy Fletcher."

"Yeah, everybody knows your name." She giggled in a very normal way, but I didn't let my guard down. There was too much weirdness around; I didn't want to be disappointed by another person. "You're our new principal's daughter, right?"

I nodded and smiled. "Yeah, that's right."

She nodded towards Michael. "Don't mind him; he's a free spirit, so he hates the hierarchy position created by the Bloods."

At that, the *free spirit* looked up to glare at her, and then went back to sleep. She grinned at me conspiratorially and I grinned back. She reminded me of Remora, who did and said things as she liked without considering the consequences of her actions. However, unlike Remora, Janet was plain. Remora was what you'd call a teenage glam.

"Well, that makes me feel better." I grinned. It was true; I felt a lot of weirdness explain by her simple sentence.

"World History is taught by Ms Butter but she gets sick easily so she rarely ever comes to class," Janet said, turning her chair around so that she was facing me properly. The girl beside her, a generic looking blonde turned as well.

"I'm Vanessa Lee," she said with a smile. "I'm guessing I don't have to introduce my parents as well?"

I nodded gratefully. "Yes, please don't."

"You're actually unlucky today," Janet whispered jokingly.

"And why is that?" I asked, curious. She waggled her eyebrows at Vanessa and Michael rolled his eyes.

"The hottest guy in school isn't here today!" she told me teasingly. "He's a Blood, but if ever I saw real beauty . . ."

They laughed and the *free spirit* even looked up to smile at me. Suddenly, it felt as if the world was right again.

34

By the time the final school bell rang, I'd made friends with the entire class. This was normal for me. This was Wendy Fletcher, the charismatic natural leader. But everything went awry when everyone got up to leave, and Snowy was waiting at the door. Conversation dried up faster than water in a dessert.

"Hello, Wendy. There's someone who wants to meet you," Snowy said casually, as if everyone else in the room didn't exist. Her amazing blue eyes sparkled when she smiled.

"Um, okay, let's go." I sighed. I tried to look at Michael, Janet and Vanessa to say bye but they'd turned into zombies, shuffling quickly out of class. So much for respect.

There was a dead silence in the hallway full of teens taking their stuff out of their lockers and heading out.

"So, who wants to meet me?" I asked, painfully aware that the silence was caused by Snowy's presence. Snowy looked thoughtful.

"I'm not sure how to tell you. He's someone you know but don't know." She frowned. "The most accurate way to explain is he's someone you knew but haven't met yet." She pressed her finger to her temple as if she had a headache.

"Are you alright?" I asked. She was looking paler than when I'd left her earlier.

She sighed. "I'll be fine once everything is back to the way it should be, when all the mix ups are cleared, when —" she stopped abruptly. She looked at me, her face getting paler. I didn't know how that was possible. She looked as white as chalk now.

"Uh, sure," I said, surprised that I pulled that off with nonchalance. "That would be best. Then you should rest, or something."

She smiled, relief flooding her face, and with it, a bit of colour. "Thanks. I can't wait for this meeting to happen."

She looked normal again, pale but Snowy pale, if you know what I mean. Excitement lifted the air and I was surprised. Was Snowy projecting her feelings? Could anyone do that?

I tried to ignore the awkward silence around me to think. There was so much amiss. Little puzzle pieces floated around my head, trying to find a connection.

Snowy, Summer and Jason were part of the Blood founding families. They had access to the school and the entire town. Only they could sit at the garden. Snowy seems to know more about me than she should. If they could access the school so easily, then it seems that Michael's points were valid. They didn't mind me being in their circle, and I don't think it has anything to do with my charisma.

How puzzling. My brow knitted. What has all this to do with me? What about my own feelings about this? Now that I thought about it, I realised that the three of them seemed familiar to me as well. I'd seen them somewhere before, but where? They all obviously knew me; they treated me as if I was an old friend, but why?

I tried to be sneaky about prying some information from Snowy. "So, if you are one of the founding families, then who else is?" I asked, making sure to put just the right amount of innocence into my question.

Snowy smiled indulgently. "Well, Summer, Jason, and me. There's another two, but they're unavailable right now. Actually, I'm taking you to see one of them."

"Okay," I said brightly. "What about adults? Any other founders?" When I asked that, I meant their parents, but then another piece fell into the already confusing puzzle. I realised that none of them had been willing to tell me their parents' names. More than that, it was as if they couldn't. Why?

Snowy's face went paler again. "Adults? Oh, they're around. They do what they have to. The founders are just us. Please don't ask any more questions." Snowy looked pained.

Ooookay.

"Okay." I mumbled, more confused than ever. I felt something pushing in my head, some info that I'm forgetting, but the more I tried to grasp it, the more elusive it became. It almost felt like I should know what was happening but was forgetting it.

What the hell?

Snowy took me to the garden, and I expected to see a guy I didn't know. It was a guy alright, but I knew him.

"Jason?" Snowy and I said simultaneously. Both of us exchanged a mystified look. I looked at Snowy because she was supposedly bringing me to someone I didn't know. She in turn looked at me, equally confused.

Jason sighed loudly, standing up to face us. He looked stressed out; the way Snowy had been really pale earlier. "I told you guys to call me Jase." He chuckled; a very weak attempt at humour. When he saw what a failure that line was, his shoulders slumped.

"He . . . can't take it." *Jase* looked at the ground. "He's not ready." I could tell that the words were directed at me, but I seriously couldn't figure them out.

"Um, yeah, okay." I realised my eloquence was really thriving. I shook my head to concentrate on the situation at hand. I wasn't going to let myself close off just because I didn't like it again. Things have gotten too strange for that. "He can have all the time he needs, whoever he is. Would anyone like to explain to me what the *hell* is going on?"

Snowy looked disappointed. "He promised," she whispered.

"His situation is such, Snowy. You have to understand," Jase said sadly. Were they ignoring me?

"Are you guys ignoring me?" I complained. I didn't want to be the whiny new kid, but the weird in this town seriously crossed the line.

"How can we ignore you? You're the whole reason why this is happening." Summer came into the garden from a side door that I'd only just noticed.

Snowy's head popped up, and she shot Summer a panicked warning look. Summer waved her concern away. She walked directly towards me, slowly, hands raised as if she was afraid I would bolt if she made an unexpected move.

I was thinking of bolting anyway.

"I'm saying this because you have to remember. We can't tell you directly, or the Ritual will be messed up, but we can give you hints." She took a deep breath and stopped right in front of me, her eyes burning into mine as if she placed a world of hope on me.

"We have waited for you for a very long time, and now that you're here, we just can't stand it anymore." Summer's voice slowly changed, as if she was going back through time, aging. "You will remember us, old friend. You know everything you should. You will return to your current abode and ponder upon my words."

I was mesmerised, looking into the fire in her dark green eyes. They were deep, and so very, very green, and . . . familiar?

"Summer, you are pushing it. Can't you feel it? We are bound!" Jason's voice broke through my reverie.

I took two quick steps back, breathing deeply. Mark, I thought desperately, I've come to a school of loons. Jason took a step towards me, and I turned and ran for my life.

I ran, feeling my bag bump against my back with every step. I put everything I had into my legs and ran towards Alex's car. But the second I was out of the building, I realised I had no idea where he'd parked his car. I cursed myself for being so rash this morning and not staying in the car until he parked it.

Thankfully, Alex was already in the car and when he saw me, he honked his loud, irritating horn. Today, the sound was a welcome one. I ran towards the car and got in quickly, slamming the door behind me.

"Go, go, go!" I panted urgently.

Alex automatically responded, and stepped on the gas, and then he looked surprised that he did that. "What's going on?" he demanded.

"Oh, nothing." I tried to breathe around the pounding of my heart. "There are just a few town-founding family members out to recruit me to a weird game of craziness."

Alex blinked, looking at me, and then turned back to face the road. "Right," he mumbled. "You want to talk about it?"

"Nope," I said, firmly. "Nope, I'm going to forget it. I'm gonna forget everything that happened today."

Alex frowned. "It wasn't so bad, was it? I had a great time."

"Good for you," I said sincerely. Not so bad? You wouldn't believe it.

Chapter 5

RECALLING THE INCREDIBLE NON-PAST

As with the week before, I slammed all the doors on my way to my room. I threw my bag against the wall, only mildly surprised when it hit a lot harder than I'd expected, and all my things burst out, spilling around the room.

This was probably what was called "releasing tension" or in my case, "showing temper" or more accurately, "throwing tantrum". I shook my head to clear my stupid thoughts, and threw myself on the bed.

What did Summer mean? What did Jason mean? What did Snowy mean? I couldn't focus on anything else but Summer's words. Remember what? What was in my head that was so important to them, that they wanted me to remember? What did Summer want me to "ponder" in my "abode"? Why was she talking like that?

It was almost as if Summer had cast a spell on me to make sure I could only think of this. A spell? Suddenly, the invisible drawer in the back of my mind shook again, this time harder than before. The thing I was supposed to remember but couldn't remember was right there, I tried to grasp it, but it evaded again.

It was driving me crazy.

Then I straightened my back. No, I refused to succumb to some girl's words. Weirdness was weirdness, and that was all this was. I felt something shift then, and Summer's words didn't seem to matter so much anymore. I shoved it to the back of my mind.

"Wendy? Honey? Are you alright?" My mother's voice called up the stairs. "I heard something loud."

"I'm fine! Just." I floundered around in my head for an idea. "I just fell!" Not very creative, I know. It didn't score high on the originality category either.

"Okay." My mom's voice called back. I could hear the doubt in her words, but she accepted the excuse. "Well, when you're done falling and messing your room, come down for tea!"

I was surprised. It was only four o' clock, and since when did we ever have tea?

It was then that I really saw what was in front of me, and groaned. The school hadn't allotted a locker for me yet, so I'd had to carry all my books around. Now, because of my mindless tantrum, the books and stationery were all strewn about my room.

I groaned twice, loudly, for good measure. My day was so perfect, it couldn't get any better. With that beautiful sarcasm in mind, I started cleaning my stuff off the floor.

By the time I went down to the kitchen, Adrienne and Alex were already halfway through the muffins and scones and tea.

"What took you so long, dear?" Adrienne asked. "I heard a lot of loud noise coming from your room."

"I just . . . fell," I grumbled sourly. I sat at a chair and picked up a chocolate muffin. "*Itadakimasu*," I said. It was a

Japanese food blessing; they always said that before eating. I sometimes said it when I felt like it. My family was really into Japanese stuff.

"You fall down in your own room too much," Adrienne said suspiciously. I just shrugged.

"I misplace a lot of things," I replied casually, nibbling the muffin and was pleasantly surprised at the richness of it. I felt my frustrations of the day rolling away like it was never there. I swear, chocolate was magic.

The muffin fell from my hands and I choked. Adrienne and Alex both stood up quickly. Alex poured a cup of tea and shoved it in my hands while Adrienne thumped on my back to get the dislodged piece loose. I tried to drink while she slammed on my back which kind of choked the piece back up.

I spluttered tea and chocolate on the table and Adrienne swiftly cleaned it up.

"What happened?" Alex looked bewildered. I shook my head and took a small sip of warm tea. It slid down my throat soothingly.

"Sorry," I croaked. "I just thought of something." Magic. Magic, magic, magic. The drawer in my mind rattled harder than before. There was something to do with magic in this huge mess.

If magic was considered, then my dreams—

The thought was cut off when Adrienne rubbed my back gently. "Feel better?"

I nodded. I picked up the chocolate muffin again, shoving the thought aside for the moment.

"We were talking about the town's history," my mom smiled. "It's very quaint. Do you want to hear about it?"

I shrugged, sincerely not sure whether I wanted to know or not. I have, after all, met three members of the founding families.

"Well, this all began very long ago. It was said that back in the time of witches and sorcerers, people were very afraid of them. So, when the human population grew, they grew bold along with the numbers. When they assumed someone was practising the Black Arts, they would tie the person up and burn them at the stake," Adrienne said.

"Well, this town was founded by five people. Their last names are different now from back then, and no one knows what their names used to be anymore,' she continued. "One of the founding members — this was before they founded the town — was deemed a witch and was burned at the stake. The people had assumed that all five were witches, but when the accused one burned without anything happening, the people realised that they had burned a human and were very contrite."

Alex took over. "The people tried to apologize to the other four but the four were distraught. Now, the five of them had been people of great wealth, and that was one of the reasons why they had been suspected. When this happened, the four used everything they had to buy out the town, the businesses, everything, and made it their own."

Alex shook his head. "Quite an impressive revenge. From then on, this town belonged to them. They called it Queenstown as tribute to their friend, the falsely accused human. Apparently, that person was everything to them. They are more of royalty than founders when it all comes down to it, because they didn't actually find the town, they owned it. All for the sake of one friend."

"How can we ignore you? You're the whole reason why this is happening."

I set my half eaten muffin down. "I don't feel well; I think I'm going to go to bed now."

Alex was surprised. He looked at the clock. "Oh my, how time flies. It's already six."

Adrienne jumped. "Oh, my! I haven't prepared dinner yet!" she exclaimed and started clearing the tea stuff off the table.

43

"Mom, the muffin was great," I said quickly, and retreated upstairs to my room, trying to keep my mind closed all the way up. When I finally stumbled into my room, I staggered towards my bed, feeling nauseous.

Then everything went black before I even hit the pillows.

*   *   *

It was a beautiful day. The sun was out and shining brightly and warm rays of light filled the meadow where I stood. There were very few clouds in the sky, and I closed my eyes, leaning my head back to feel the sun on my face. A gentle, sweet smelling breeze lifted my long hair. I smiled at the simplicity of it all.

"Crescentia!"

I heard my friends calling out for me. I waited there for them to find me. I wanted them to feel all this wondrous freedom as well.

"Crescentia, where are you?" Ah, that would be Gwenwyn. The little grandmother. She would worry about everything, that one, despite how small she was.

"It is so like her," Ezra's voice grumbled. "To go missing when we want her." I almost took offense at his words but there was a fondness there that was impossible to miss. I smiled at their worry, feeling quite cheeky about it.

"Crescentia! Crescentia!" That was Quinteth, and I considered showing myself. She was so mature that it made me feel like a child to play with them this way.

"Let her be," *his* soothing voice said. "She knows we are here. Let us just embrace this good weather. It is but a small meadow, we will chance upon her in no time."

I smiled. Oh, how well he knew me. And he was right; within the next few moments, they found me.

They ran forward to me, relief flooding their faces.

"What are you doing here?" his beautiful face was open, inquiring. I smiled calmly.

"I am enjoying this." I pointed towards the sky. Then I pointed towards the tall flowers amongst us. The meadow was so full of them that I couldn't see any ground.

They smiled at me and closed their eyes, enjoying it all as well.

Everything was so beautiful at that moment that I was surprised when I was hit by anxiety. Their eyes opened to look at me simultaneously.

This is different than usual. It was powerful. I bent forward, retching, sinking to my knees, flowers flooding my face. My heart was hit over and over by a dark wave of anxiety. They crowded around me, concerned. My beautiful one pushed them further back to give me space and he knelt beside me, holding me up.

The moment passed as suddenly as it came.

I stood up straight, as if that had never occurred. "Something bad is coming. I don't know what, but it is big. It is very big this time."

They stood around me in silence. We all pondered on what this may mean.

"Let us cleanse our home." I decided. "Purifying seems to be the most important thing at a time like this."

They nodded mutely, sober with the grim situation. I turned my face to the sun one last time. I reached up and collected the light.

O great light of heat,
Grant now power for one feat,
Cast shadow into shadow,
Keep sweet light in such meadow.

I dropped my hands and smiled, feeling the sun flood the meadow, where the power of light was absorbed. There was nothing more I could do for this place. It would be healthy forever.

My beautiful one held my hand and we went to our tower.

At the tower, I could feel the ominous future looming. I shivered. We started running inside. The sky was turning dark too quickly, and I saw dark clouds covering the brightness. It was a bad omen. We ran up the steps to our highest room where we performed our Rituals.

"Ezra, close the door!" I ordered. "Quinteth, draw the pentagram! Gwenwyn, bring me chamomile, lavender and sage! Alpheus, arrange the candles!"

I took a light jump, and flew lightly to the window. There was a thunderstorm raging. Too fast, too fast, everything was moving too fast. I stabbed a finger to the clouds.

"*Disperse!*" I called, my voice ringed with power. The clouds instantly obeyed, drifting apart and lightening. It would not hold long, for I didn't use words of power. I just had to disperse them quickly for I needed a clear sky.

"It is ready, Crescentia!" Alpheus called to me urgently, his beautiful voice reminding me to focus.

Time to think later, Crescentia. His voice was in my head and I nodded at him.

I stepped into the middle of the drawn pentagram. We only had to draw one. I had created it such that we can invoke any spell upon this one. The others stepped around the pentagram at their appointed positions. They had surrounded the pentagram with candles and they each held one.

"*Light!*" I demanded, and the candles lighted up in purple flames, my trademark colour. I picked up the plants at my feet.

"White sage of white mage, white prevails with all white might." I burned the sage at Alpheus's candle, moving quickly around the circle, to Gwenwyn, to Quinteth, to Ezra. Once I had burnt the sage on all their candles, I picked up the chamomile.

"White leaf of white mage, white calms with all white might." I did the same thing with the chamomile. The storm that had been coming back slowed drastically. I didn't waste any time. I picked up the lavender.

"Coloured flower, coloured power, take the might, obtain the power." I burnt the lavender stalk in turn again. I felt power being drawn from me, from my friends, from the sage and chamomile. The lavender scent lifted into the artificially created wind, bringing with it all the power invoked and spreading it throughout the region.

The very walls of the tower were cleansed through and the power spread out across the lands, spreading and spreading until the entire country was cleanst. But that wasn't all. I felt the power and I felt what it had cleanst.

"It is finished. Thank you." I stepped out of the pentagram and the drawing vanished. The purple flames were all extinguished at once, and my friends slumped to the floor, breathing hard. They were not as powerful as me, so the effects they felt were more draining, even though most of it was my power.

"The humans are searching again," I said, annoyed. "They never give up. I sometimes admire that trait. However, the ones that died were all human as well. The falsely accused. As much as I like humans, I can't stand it when they commit senseless murder."

"They cannot be blamed, Crescentia, and you know it." Alpheus calmed me with a touch to my shoulder. "They have been through many terrible situations. Not all of those in our power are white mages."

I nodded. "I know."

Then the five of us laughed awkwardly to release our tension.

We went out of the tower to find a mob waiting for us. I was shocked. How did I not sense them? The intent on their faces was obvious to anyone with eyes. They held torches and masks. There was a type of gas released into the air and one by one, blackness claimed us and we dropped like stone.

I opened my eyes and found myself bound to a stake. No! Fear claimed me and I shook.

"Tis' a witch!" A man screamed. An uproar rose in the crowd surrounding me from a distance.

"Burn the witch!"

"Kill the dark creature!"

Cries rose from the people. I tried to speak, but to no avail. There was a cloth upon my mouth. Oil was poured on my person, thrown by the humans.

"Cast your torches!" called another man. "If your family has been wronged by witches, *cast your torches*!"

Torches flew towards me, one hitting me right on the face, bringing the cloth down from the force. I was about to protest when I felt it. The raging fire upon my feet brought tremendous pain. My protest transformed into a cry of pain.

The fire caught quickly on the oil on my dress and I burned. I couldn't bear the agony. I screamed as the fire consumed me. The pain filled my mind, released through my cries. My magic was feebly trying to extinguish the fire, but it was pointless. I could feel my power, but the pain was in the way. All my power could do was to heal my burning flesh.

The sickening smell of my own flesh searing filled the air. Unbearable. I shrieked in high pitch, holding the note for a long time as the pain licked at my body.

Then I felt them. My friends were using their amazing power to boost their speed, and they were running towards me. It put things into clarity and I was in touch with my magic again, access to infinite power.

I wanted so badly to kill all these humans so that I may rejoin my friends. Then I saw his face. The most beautiful face in the world. Alpheus. He was staring at me in absolute horror, his face bone-white.

Seeing his face reminded me of his words this afternoon. I couldn't blame them. And this time, they got a real witch. So instead of using my power to destroy the humans, I used it to keep my friends away.

However, there was only so much a great witch could do. My power had been slighted by the cleansing spell, and sending the barrier was eating up my power reserves. I sent it as far as it would go, and Alpheus was pushed backwards.

His eyes widened once he realised what I was doing and he shook his head fiercely, looking at me in such bewildered pain that I almost did what I first wanted to do. The magic couldn't keep the barrier and heal me at the same time anymore, not without words of power.

And somehow, I knew my time was up. This was it. After protecting humans for millennia, they were going to kill me, and I was letting them. The pain that had been building exploded and I released an intensely bloodcurdling scream.

His beautiful face was haggard, as if he'd lost all his life with that scream. Then, just before my life slipped away, I gave him the sweetest smile that ever I could manage. Let him remember me as the most powerful witch that gave up her life for the humans.

"I love you," I mouthed and his eyes widened.

Just like that, I was gone.

Chapter 6

REUNITED AND DEADLY

I slowly became aware again from my slumber. I kept my eyes closed, trying to process the new information. Or rather, old information. I remember everything now. What am I to do? I can already feel our consciousness's melting together. Unfortunately for me, the Wendy me, Crescentia was overpowering.

There was a change in my body then. I felt a small searing between my shoulder blades and knew that my phoenix insignia was returning. Everything about my feelings changed and melted away. As I slowly opened my eyes, my priorities lined up clearly.

"Alpheus."

That was right. He was the most important one right now. I sat up slowly. I saw light streaming in through my window. I was Crescentia again, but I was also Wendy. My brow furrowed. This will be a bit more complicated than I had thought.

Then . . . what about Mark? I bit my lip. As much as I loved Mark, it felt more like sibling love when compared to Alpheus. I'd always known, in the back of my mind, that if there was a chance that the boy in my dreams was real, I'd drop anyone and anything for him.

And now I know that he is real. He is so very real. I took a pause in my thoughts.

"I'm so sorry, Mark."

That was it.

"Wendy! Wake up or you'll be late for school!" Adrienne called up the stairs. I went to open my room door and a welcoming smell of waffles filled the air. For a moment I was a young girl in a modern world again, but that moment passed and I felt my responsibilities weigh down on me again. I am no longer just Wendy. I am also Crescentia, the greatest witch in the history of the world.

I realised what this town meant. It means I had saved my friends, but it also uncovered something sinister. Then I laughed.

My friends, what ridiculous names you have come up with. Snowy, Summer, and Jase indeed.

I took a quick shower and packed my school bag.

"Wendy!"

"Yeah, I'm coming!" I called back. I took one last look in the mirror before heading down. I looked exactly like I used to. I smiled and saw the smile I used to see reflected back at me in lakes. So this is what it means to be reincarnated.

I turned and descended the stairs.

I noticed my parents giving me weird looks and they kept exchanging glances. It probably had something to do with my changed aura. When I awakened, my powers that had been suppressed by my mind had also awakened and I had changed considerably. I guess it showed.

When Alex dropped me off at the school entrance and went to park, I saw them waiting for me. They must have felt my change last night. The three of them stood in a line, in position. Ezra, or *Jase* in between the girls with Gwenwyn, or *Snowy* on the right and Quinteth, or *Summer* on the left.

I stood in front of them and smiled. "Well, now. I see none of you have changed at all." They stared at me, frozen, as if they couldn't believe what they were hearing. I smiled warmly.

I went to Gwenwyn and held her at arm's length. She looked exactly the same as she used to, except the modern clothes. "Gwenwyn, you look well! Quite the same, actually."

Gwenwyn's eyes filled with tears. "C-c-cres—"

I nodded. "That is right. I am back, I remember everything."

There was a beat of silence.

Then they all burst into tears and ran forward, enveloping me in a tight hug. I tripped on a small rock and we went tumbling to the ground. We lay there, giggling senselessly as relief and joy filled the air. There was such a sweet breeze that we were reluctant to rise.

"Okay, glad to see you're making friends, but this is weird, Wendy." Alex's face appeared over us and we quickly sat up.

"Erm, we were just . . ." there was really nothing that could explain our behaviour, so I let my sentence trail off. I remembered my power, and I stood up, looking Alex in the eye.

"*We were not doing anything unusual,*" I told him, coating my voice with a layer of magic. Alex's eyes glowed for a moment and then returned to normal.

"Get to class, kids," Alex said, forgetting about our floor situation.

"Wow," I giggled. I helped them up and we looked at each other. "Founding family, huh?" I grinned. "Oh, yes, where is Alpheus?"

They looked at each other nervously.

"What?" I inquired.

"He's at the garden waiting for you. None of us know what to do, or how to re-introduce him to you," Gwenwyn said. They looked down, shame-faced.

I laughed. "Oh, my friends, you are such joys to have. There is no need to overthink this."

I'd know from the moment I stepped into the school that this was our meadow. This place used to be our big meadow, and my friends have built a school on top of it. I wondered why, and made a mental note to ask them later.

I walked purposefully towards the garden, and realised that it was where I'd spelled the place for sunlight. Ah, no wonder they were so protective over the place. I bit my lip to hide my smile. And there it was; his presence. He could feel me, too. I couldn't wait to see his beautiful face again, and I ran forward.

And I saw him. Love and joy burst through my heart and I ran forward. Alpheus stood quickly and we stood at arm's length, just staring into each other's face. His pale golden hair floated lightly in the warm breeze and my heart went into frenzy. I never thought I'd see my precious angel's face again.

His beautiful eyes, his beautiful face, were finally within my reach. Calm radiated throughout my body and I took a step towards him. His eyes absorbed the movement, he himself not moving. There was a deep emotion in his eyes, and I felt the bewilderment that he was feeling.

I wrapped my arms around him tightly, feeling comforted by the familiarity of his muscles. "Alpheus," I whispered.

That was when he broke down. His arms went around me tightly, his broken sobs shaking us both. Waves upon waves of pain flooded our bodies and I realised that being separated from me caused him such incredible pain. I tightened my hold on him.

I am here now, I told him in my mind. *We are together again. I love you!*

Yes, as I love you, He was filled with joy and relished the feel of holding me in his arms again.

The meadow intercepted our feelings, absorbing them, and glowed. Everything glowed brilliantly. My friends joined us and we just stayed there, reliving our memories again. By the time the bell rang, we were seated on the benches facing the fountain. Alpheus sat on the same bench as me. We held hands, either one unwilling to let go.

We're all smiling. We had no idea what to say, but just being near each other again was utter bliss. I recalled back in Crescentia's day, we were all content to just lie in our meadow for hours on end. But there was trouble impending, and I couldn't just ignore it anymore.

"There is trouble," I sighed. All of their eyes, already trained on my face, widened. "It wasn't a coincidence."

They instinctively knew what I was talking about. They nodded uneasily, waiting for me to continue. Alpheus was the only one whose expression remained unchanged, as if he'd known as much.

"I didn't sense the humans, so it is obvious that they had been Shielded from my Sight. The humans back then didn't have the technology or intelligence to create sleeping gas, so it was a spell," I said my deductions aloud. They closed their eyes and absorbed my reasoning. I resisted the urge to smile. It had been too long since we last did this.

"They only took me, so I was considered a threat, but not you. This narrows it down to witches or warlocks that are less or equally powerful to me, but more powerful than you," I continued. "The humans apologized to you after thinking that I'm human, means they were under a glamour spell; they did not know what they were doing."

"Now the only questions left are who and why." Alpheus finished for me in his beautiful voice. I smiled at him and nodded delightfully.

"Correct." I congratulated him gleefully.

Ezra rolled his eyes. "Only you, Crescentia, are able to smile while discussing your murderer. Talk about happy-go-lucky."

Alpheus remained calm, as usual. He hadn't changed at all. He still carried that amazing aura that projected calm security. Alpheus will always be the rock in my life. He looked at me and smiled, reading my thoughts towards him.

As are you, Crescentia, he thought.

"She is simplicity in joy itself, I think." Gwenwyn laughed. "The pinnacle of good form."

"Don't talk about me like I'm not here," I scolded playfully. "But this is quite funny. We have all adapted to the modern world," I giggled.

Alpheus chuckled quietly, amused at my amusement.

"When do you intend to search out this murderer?" Quinteth asked. Ever the mature one, serious in the face of calamity.

"Hmmm . . . Never?" I tried. As I had thought, the word didn't sit well with any of them.

A protest rose in the air, all of them arguing about what I should and should not do. The biggest protest came from Alpheus's silence, his mouth turned down and the air grew heavy from his disapproval.

"Well, I am here now, and that is all that matters, right?" I insisted. "If the evil one doesn't know I have been reborn, then I don't want to alert it to the fact."

Alpheus sighed. "You know why," he told me quietly, and he was right. I was being selfish with my request. If an evil one wanted me out of the way, then there must be a reason, or some form of catastrophe. We couldn't just sit around and do nothing about that, especially since I am back now.

"Very well." I bit my lip. "Where is our temple now?"

We had previously used the highest room in our tower as our temple to perform our Rituals. Now, I didn't know where they had moved it to.

"It is at my house," Alpheus said. "In the attic."

"How high is that?" I wondered aloud. Height was important. The higher, the better.

"Not very, it is only above the second storey in my house," Alpheus said. I frowned. A second storey house attic wasn't an ideal place for a temple.

"Is there any church here?" I fired my questions. Churches were good for temples because they were holy places. "You guys bought the entire town, where is our tower? Is there any building that is as high as our previous temple?"

They looked at one another in subtle agitation.

"We couldn't keep the tower; not without revealing what we were," Ezra said sourly.

There was an obvious question mark on my face.

"Because it is an old building, we were pressured to either tear it down for development or open it for tourism. We couldn't keep our temple for fear it would be discovered," Quinteth explained. "So we tore it down."

"The highest building would have to be the church," Gwenwyn said. "But it is not much taller than a three storey house."

I frowned. "What then? It is not good enough. How have you been performing the Rituals?"

They looked down sheepishly. Even Alpheus? How very odd.

"We . . . performed them anyway," Quinteth said guiltily, taking on the responsibility by admitting the truth. It must have been on her suggestion then. She never sounded guilty unless she was truly in the wrong.

I slapped my forehead. "What!" I exclaimed. "All of you performed our Rituals only three storeys from the ground!" I was devastated. "You are well aware of the consequences of this!"

I looked at Alpheus, the one I thought I could always depend on.

"Do *not* look at the ground with shame on your faces," I said fiercely. "If you did this, look at me and apologize the correct way. I will *not* allow us to fall apart now."

They looked at each other and resolve shone in their eyes. They turned to me and stood, then went down on one knee.

"We apologize, Great One," they said as one. I hated it when they had to apologize, because I hated being reminded that they were inferior to me. But I only ever made them apologize when they have committed a grave sin. Performing magic so close to the earth would have created major problems. I would not be surprised if the increased natural disasters all around the world were because of them.

"You are forgiven," I said, and they released a sigh of relief. "But trust will only be restored after penance." They tensed. The penances that I dished out were never easy, but it was always to teach them a lesson.

"*This is your penance, heed my words,*" I spread my arms out, as was the norm for penance Rituals. "*Build a tower of high number.*"

They bowed lower and felt the binding power flow over them. It galled me to see them bow, especially when they are my friends. Tears flowed down my face.

57

"*We heed,*" they replied, they voices coated with the binding spell.

I dropped my hands. "Why do you insist on making me do this?" I fell to my knees and picked them up. As a Great White Mage, I have Bound them to me, which meant that they were to obey my words, and I would be compelled to dish out punishments when my commands had been compromised. As they were Bound into submission, I was Bound into authority.

Alpheus looked at me and smiled. "Because you don't act like what you are. We need to be reminded once in a while who is in power."

They laughed, the entire event already forgotten. Alpheus smiled at me softly, wiping my tears away with his thumb. I sighed.

"You guys seriously cannot be saved." I rolled my eyes. "We can build a tower here, and use the founding member's privilege as a reason. But we should treat the humans here well. I don't want a repeat of events from my past life," I said, remembering Michael's discontentment.

They nodded as one in agreement.

"Come now, we should go to class," I said. They groaned, and I was surprised. "I thought we all loved learning?"

"Do you know how many centuries we spent learning? The humans' syllabus is ridiculous!" Gwenwyn exclaimed. "They change it as they like, and the history all around the world is different. If we weren't alive in that time, we would have been fooled as well."

"I see," I muttered, realising that all the lessons I'd had as Wendy was false. "It is alright, we must leave things as they are. Now, to class. Our teachers await." I declared dramatically.

Chapter 7

REBUILDING AND MAKING AMENDS

When I walked into the Chemistry lab, everyone looked up at me like they did yesterday and froze, their eyes sliding over to Alpheus, who came in with me. Then they looked down at their books. Even the teacher stared for a moment and then looked away. Silence rose awkwardly.

I resisted the urge to roll my eyes. "Teach," I told the teacher, and then I held on to Alpheus and dragged him to the two empty seats at the back. We sat close together and held hands under the table.

The teacher looked at me, obviously at war with himself. I tuned into his mind.

Should I ask her to introduce herself? He fretted. *But there is a Blood with her. Would that be disrespectful?*

I groaned internally and stood up. "Wendy Fletcher, daughter of Alex Fletcher and Adrienne Fletcher." Then I sat back down to round two of awkward silence.

"Teach," Alpheus repeated what I said. A cold breeze filled the room. I noticed a few students shivered and the teacher quickly looked at me with a forced smile.

"I am Mr Paul." He introduced himself to me and quickly immersed himself into the lesson.

What is your undercover name? I asked Alpheus in my mind. He instantly knew what I meant.

Corey, he told me. I bit my lip to resist laughing. He nudged me indignantly, but he was smiling as well.

I can't help it. From Alpheus to Corey?

Well, what about your name? Wendy?

The difference is that I didn't name myself. I looked at him from under my lashes and gave him a cheeky smile. He pursed his lips.

Well, if you were to change your name, what would you choose? He asked, and there was real curiosity behind his joking façade. I thought about it.

Hmmm. That is a hard question. I tried to think of what name I would give myself if I had to change my name like them. *Kelly?* I thought of the friends I had in Settleburg City. Definitely not Remora. Only Remora was Remora. *Rachel?*

Those names are so generic, he told me mockingly. *Come on, you can do better than that Crescentia.*

I bit my lip, running all the girl's names I knew in my mind, trying to find one that would suit me.

How about . . . then I grinned. Ah. I have a good one. *Elizabeth?*

Alpheus scrutinised my face, keeping that name in his mind, trying to see the fit. *Not bad. You should have been named Elizabeth.*

Thank you. I shot him a smug, triumphant smile.

Do you want me to call you Elizabeth? Or I can nickname you Beth, the way humans always shorten names?

Yeah, now he was totally mocking me. I dug my elbow into his ribs but that only made him chuckle quietly.

A few people were curious; I could feel their emotions targeting us. I muttered a quick spell to make their interest wane, and their curiosity instantly dried up. Alpheus had noticed as well, but he didn't think much of it.

Not Beth, then. Lizzy?

I groaned internally. *What is this?*

I'm going to make up for lost time, Crescentia. His soothing voice flowed through my mind. I leaned into his side and closed my eyes. I felt my heart race and heard my blood pound in my ears from our proximity.

Then don't speak. I replied. He put his strong chin lightly on my head and we closed our eyes.

Curiosity sparked up again, and I ignored it this time. We stayed that way for the entire class, just relishing in the feel of being close.

When the bell rang, we left before the others as they kept silent. Hmmm, I was going to have to do something about that. I don't want Michael and everyone else to be unhappy about the *respect* we were getting.

Who is Michael? Alpheus wondered. I looked at him.

Seriously?

He nodded sheepishly. Wow, two sheepish looks in a day from Alpheus Di Namphazar. This was surely a record. He sighed because he felt my disappointment in him. How could he, Alpheus, be ignorant to the people around him?

"I could not concentrate on others," he said sadly. He wasn't making excuses; it was just true. I tightened my hold on his hand, regretting my disappointment.

"It is alright, Alpheus." I said sweetly, wanting to erase all the pain I'd caused by leaving.

"I am Corey, remember?" He smiled ruefully at me.

That's the spirit.

"There you are!" Gwenwyn's voice echoed through the silent hallway. She ran to catch up to us with Quinteth and Ezra trailing behind.

We stood in a circle, but realised quickly that we were inconveniencing the others around us, so we ended up in the garden again.

"I would like to name this place," I commented, breathing in the fresh air. "Quinteth, you name it."

She beamed at me, glad to have something to do. "I will think about it."

"Now, Gwenwyn, what is it?" I turned to the naturally pale girl. The name 'Snowy' had suited her uncannily. "I have, uh, spoken to the school board, and they would love to have a tower, except that we don't have that much expense anymore." Gwenwyn sighed. "Schools are not quite profitable investments, I'm afraid."

"Use my wealth," I said. I knew they would not have touched my money without my permission. They are Bound, the way I am, but differently.

Alpheus nodded. "Is it practical, though, to have a tower in the school grounds, where anybody can have access to it?"

"Oh, that's right." I wanted to do a face palm. "Is there any open space that is under your names? You are the founders of this town, aren't you?"

Ezra nodded. "There are two small parks. We can use one as our personal space and build our tower, and widen the other to compensate for it."

I nodded. "That is a very good idea. I need to give the town something, though. The humans are unhappy with the hierarchy system."

They all frowned except Alpheus, who maintained his calm face as per usual. I was secretly relieved, for I was worried that he had changed.

"The humans," Ezra said in disgust. "They —"

I held up a hand to silence him. I felt some presence approaching. They were students.

62

"*Wind of hearing, silent breathing, contain the words and give deaf odds,*" I said the words of power to make our garden soundproof. A small wind flared up and blew at the edges of the garden, keeping our words inside.

"They . . . ?" I asked, prompting Ezra to continue.

"They are so selfish!" Ezra vented with a passion. I felt his fury and hatred towards them, and knew without a doubt that it was because of me. "They kill you, and you want to give them things? Whatever for?"

"Remember, Ezra, it is not their fault." Quinteth tried to say it neutrally but I could hear the bitter resentment in her voice as well. What have I done? I despaired. Because of my one decision, I had left my friends alone for centuries and they had harboured hate towards humans because of it. How will I ever make this right?

"Inner cleansing spell," I muttered. "We must perform the Ritual soon. The hate in your hearts will make it hard to perform proper Rituals."

They nodded in agreement, and I had the vague feeling that they had experienced some awry Rituals. Oh dear, there was much to do.

"How soon can the tower be built?" I queried.

"In a month," Gwenwyn replied.

"So soon?" I was surprised. I knew from Wendy's knowledge that it took quite long to build buildings.

"Because I kept our own tower's design, and there are already builders in town," Gwenwyn explained. I smiled. That's right, she's the little grandmother.

"This town doesn't have builders of its own?" I wondered aloud.

All of them shook their heads.

"We rent them from the Royal City," Quinteth explained. "Our town's people are mainly farmers, woodcutters and fishermen, because our soil is incredibly healthy, thanks to you."

I blinked. "What?"

"Your Sun spell, remember? You caught the sun and kept it in the ground," Ezra reminded me.

Oh, that's right.

"I see." I grinned merrily. "My legacy, is it?"

I sat down at one of the benches and they followed suit. We just sat there in companionable silence.

"Avalon." Quinteth blurted suddenly.

We started at her abrupt outburst and looked at her strangely.

"Sorry?" Ezra said.

"The name of the garden," Quinteth said, awe slowly dawning on her face. "Avalon Garden."

"It's perfect!" Gwenwyn laughed. Ezra gave Quinteth a congratulatory tap on the shoulder, and Alpheus and I looked at each other in amazement. It really was perfect. The name rang sweetly in the air, as if the garden itself has accepted the name.

We spent the day in Avalon, and they made me tell every little detail of life as Wendy, and I registered that none of them liked Remora or Mark, and it had something to do with jealousy. I kept my amusement to myself.

Then I made them tell me everything that they had been through since my departure, and that ate through more than four hours of school time. They even explained to me how they kept searching for my essence, and waiting for me to come back, and how they started planning everything to perfection once they found where I was. Sometime halfway through must have been recess time, because Gwenwyn left and came back with food for everyone, and peach juice for me.

When the end of school bell rang, we were all at the front gate, waiting for my dad to pick me up. In a way, it was very strange, I was Crescentia, yet I was Wendy at the same time. As a witch of many millennia, I could still recall my original parents. As the reincarnation of myself, I have a modern family now. I felt sad that I was the only one of us with a family now.

Alex came out from the principal's office and nodded at me, holding up a hand to wave at the others, and then pointed to his car.

"He wants me to wait here for him while he gets his car," I explained to them, because they looked puzzled by the gestures.

"How does it feel to be older than your parents?" Ezra quipped cheekily. Quinteth elbowed him in the ribs, and we all chuckled.

"Correction, I am not older than them, as I was truly just reborn," I said. "I can no longer pride myself on being an Old One, though as far as I know, my powers are the same."

They nodded, accepting the words in silence. We were all used to me being the oldest one that it was hard to adjust to the fact that I am now four centuries younger than them.

Alex's car drove up, and he rolled down the window. "Anyone needs a lift home?" he offered. They politely declined and waved goodbye to me as I entered the car.

There was silence in the car for a few minutes.

"So, are you hanging out with the Bloods now?" Alex asked curiously. He must have picked up the name for them from the teachers. I shrugged.

"They are very nice people." I realised that I needed to be more of Wendy around him. "I think they've accepted me into their group. Cool, huh?"

He snorted. "Well, you were always Mrs Big Shot." We both laughed, and I secretly wondered if he knew how true those words were.

When we reached home, I showered quickly, inhaled my food, and then spent the rest of the day putting all our building plans into detail.

For the rest of the month, it was a whirlwind of activity. We planned school parties and I forced the Bloods to try to talk to the other students, and the effects were seen almost immediately. It was as though the students had admired the Bloods and had only wanted to be acknowledged by them.

There were no longer pressing silences in their presence. In fact, the school grew a lot more merry and bright. The plans for the tower went well, and true to her word, Gwenwyn had the tower built within a month. As expected, there was a rumble of dissent throughout the townsfolk, but when they saw the park that we had renovated for them, all complaints vanished without a trace.

I had joined the cheerleading squad in honour of Wendy's expertise, and honestly, the squad needed my help. Unsurprisingly, I was nominated cheer captain, but I gave the spot back to Sandra Matthews, the blonde captain who accepted it with grace. I became the co-captain instead. I couldn't help noticing that all the girls in school had a thing for Alpheus, and it annoyed me at the same time it made me proud.

A week after the tower was built, we had chosen a theme for the school dance which was to be held in two weeks' time. The theme was Halloween, because the date of the dance was All Hallows Eve, the day before Halloween. Besides, how else did we get to dress up as witches?

We now stood at the highest room in the tower, and they were watching me go through the stuff. I saw a lot of pentagram drawings.

"We couldn't use your pentagram after you . . . left. The magic was anchored by you alone, because it was your creation." Quinteth explained.

Gwenwyn took over. "But we took the actual pentagrams for each particular Ritual, and it seems more effective and less tiring."

I nodded. "That's because they were made purposely for the particular spells. My pentagram generalised them, so it was less accurate and more draining, but it saves a lot of time, and we all know that time is of main essence when it comes to Rituals," I explained. I wondered why I had never explained this before. I never knew that my departure would stop my pentagram from working.

"Come, now. It is time for our cleansing Ritual."

We set the things aside and Gwenwyn drew the cleansing pentagram.

"Candles, white sage, rosemary and lavender," I said. I noticed that they were fighting to keep the smiles of their faces when they heard my orders. Yeah, it was good to be back.

We performed our cleansing Ritual and I could virtually feel the town shedding its old skin and waking up. The spell also refreshed the townsfolk and a positive energy radiated throughout the town lightly. Ah, this was always the good part.

We smiled at each other. Yeah, it was really good to be back.

Chapter 8

ALL THE DAMN PARADOXES

"I see your powers have increased," I mused. They didn't look very tired even though we had just casted a medium scale cleansing Ritual. Cleansing Rituals were always terribly draining.

They nodded.

"We have grown with time," Quinteth explained.

"But not nearly as much as we would have if—" Ezra stopped in mid-sentence. A heavy silence filled the air.

"If I had been here," I finished for him. I noticed Gwenwyn level a dark gaze at Ezra and I shook my head. "It is true, after all."

I looked around the tower room. It wasn't exactly the same as the previous one. It was built more proportionally, more perfectly, yet I missed the old one. And then I remembered why we needed the tower back urgently in the first place.

"You don't seem too tired, but I will not push it," I said. "We will perform our tracking spell tomorrow." I didn't like what I was saying, because I needed to find the dark mage as soon as possible. I'd been feeling a flutter of anxiety in my heart ever since I remembered my past life. The anxiety had everything to do with a few dark presences I'd been feeling throughout the regions.

"Tomorrow?" Ezra said, surprised. The others looked surprised as well.

"We can do it by today," Alpheus said in his quiet way. "Perhaps this evening."

I thought about it. For Alpheus to say it, then it must be alright. For them to be well by this evening after the spell; they have really come a long way. However, I wasn't going to take any chances and shook my head.

"Tonight, we will perform our Moon Ritual," I said, in a way that left them doubtless that there will be no arguing. They nodded, accepting my judgement, trusting me to know what's best.

A Moon Ritual was a ritual that we perform using only the full moon. It was performed to harness the power of light in the midst of darkness, to keep more of our power on reserve so that we could use more in times of distress. I was worried about their power reserves because they were unable to perform this Ritual without me. *What have I done?* I felt sad at all the handicaps I have given them. It was a wonder that they still wanted to be Bound to me. Well, it's not like they had a choice; once a witch was Bound, there was no turning back.

There were only two options, and you chose the better one, Alpheus promised me. I nodded without looking at him. I knew that was true, yet I couldn't help feeling guilty.

"Dinner at my house?" Quinteth invited brightly, ever the mature one; she probably wanted to do something to lift the heavy atmosphere that had hung upon us. I groaned out loud.

"It's Alex's birthday!" I exclaimed. "I totally forgot about it, and I have no idea what to get for him!" I looked at them pleadingly. "You guys, come over and celebrate with me please, I don't want to do it alone!"

They looked at each other, and it was easy to guess what they were thinking.

"He indulges in booze on his birthday."

That said, they instantly put themselves to work to arrange a great, booze-free party.

*   *   *

"Wow!" Alex breathed, looking around him a few hours later. I had gotten Adrienne to help us get Alex out of the house so that we could work our magic (no, not literally).

The house was decorated nicely with light flowers and the furniture had been move around to make room on the floor. We had gotten a Japanese style table and mats that we had to sit on the floor on. Alex was wild on Japanese stuff and he loved sushi as much as he loved breathing. The table was big and wide, and there were loads of raw slices of tuna and salmon and other sashimi.

"This is amazing!" Alex praised in admiration. He couldn't take his eyes off the food. "This would go well with saké!"

We cringed at each other.

"Uh, dad, we prepared green tea," I put in quickly.

He frowned for a moment and we all held our breath, and even Adrienne crossed her fingers.

"That's right! The green tea is really calming, right?" he grinned merrily and all of us suppressed sighs of relief. Then he noticed the sofa. Or rather, he noticed the big pile of presents on the sofa. "What's that!" He practically squealed with excitement.

"I just happened to have a slip of the tongue and maybe let some people know that it's your birthday today." I smiled innocently, neglecting to mention the "It's Our Principal's Birthday Today!" posters on every available space on the school walls. It was now being taken down by a well-paid-bribed janitor.

"Seriously? The people of this town are really something." He nodded at my friends. "Good job, you guys, thanks."

I motioned with my hands towards the table. "Shall we?"

For the next three hours, Alex was having the time of his life. Ezra showed off his farcical sense of humour that was seriously unhealthy for mealtimes because it almost had us rolling on the floor. Seeing as we were already sitting on the floor, it wasn't easy resisting the urge.

We cleaned up after dinner and watched Alex open his presents.

"I feel like a small kid at Christmas." He chuckled with mirth. We took turns handing him his presents and we felt very gratified watching him love our little party. Then once all the gifts had been opened, we left my parents in our living room watching a rented DVD.

I stretched and smiled happily. "Thank you so much, guys," I said to them.

"Hey, no problem." Ezra grinned. "I got to exercise my humour."

Quinteth rolled her eyes. "Yeah, okay."

Gwenwyn laughed at them, and Alpheus put an arm around my shoulder. I smiled at how modern they were being.

"Come, it is almost midnight," I said excitedly. This would be my first time doing a Moon Ritual as a reincarnation. I was curious to see if that factor affected anything.

We crossed the street and made our way over to the park with our tower. It took about twenty minutes and we reached with only five minutes to spare. The best thing about the Moon Ritual was that our power wasn't needed. It was purely to replenish our own power.

"Quick!" I whispered. "Stand in our circle."

We stood around and looked at each other. We weren't standing in our tower, but it was better this way, because this spell didn't need height. We stood with me in the middle and they made a circle around me. I turned my head up to the moon and felt the buzzing power of the sun's light being reflected by the moon. I started the chant of the first stanza.

"White rock yonder blaze,
With white light lightly glaze,
Bring forth subtle light,
Fill white mages with pure light"

We closed our eyes simultaneously, feeling the moon's light float over us and hover all around us. Alpheus moved on with the second stanza.

"White of light, of power soft
Fill the heart, white ever loft
Darkness fading, cast aside
Keep in power of white tide"

The moon's power seeped into our skins, and I knew that if I looked, we would all be glowing; our skins would be as pale as the moon.

Just as Gwenwyn was about to chant her part, which was a repetition of my stanza, I felt another presence coming. I detached a piece of my mind to check it out. The other person's consciousness was transparent, as if it wasn't really there physically. It was a mind probe, I realised. Only sorcerers and witches were able to send mind probes.

I was searched deeper and realised that it was heading towards us. Someone was looking for us. Then I was yanked back into my head by the anxiety attacks I had whenever something bad was going to happen. It was an evil presence. It was a dark mage.

"Stop, everyone, stop!" I said quickly. Their eyes snapped open and the glow from their skins faded. *"Dark of night, cloak our light."* I coated my words with power and we were Shielded. That meant that the presence won't be able to find us no matter what; it would be as if we weren't there.

We waited in silence, waiting for it to pass. I bit my lip, feeling the dark presence come closer, searching. I felt a jolt, as if the owner of the mind probe cussed, unable to find us. Then the presence waned slowly as the probe unravelled, hanging on as long as possible before disintegrating completely. I breathed a sigh of relief and Unshielded us.

"What was that?" Gwenwyn muttered. They had felt the presence as well, when it had come very close to us. There was even a point where it flowed through us, but detected nothing.

"A mind probe," I said, and frowned. Mind probes weren't good. Even sorcerers and witches of Alpheus's level couldn't conjure a mind probe. To think that there was such a powerful adversity made me worry. This was out of their hands. Only I could deal with this. Then I put two and two together and realised just how bad it was.

"They know," I whispered in fear. "They know that I've been reincarnated. But how?" *They must have been tracking for me for as long as my friends have.*

"We have to leave, don't we?" Quinteth asked. "To go somewhere we've never been so that we would be untraceable. But where?"

"We have lived for millennia; I do not think there is a place we haven't been," Gwenwyn whispered nervously.

"You guys, I can't leave," I spoke up. "I have Alex and Adrienne to look after. They are my parents."

"Perhaps you could suggest moving?" Ezra offered. I shook my head.

"They won't move because I ask them to. My powers will have little or no effect on them because I have their blood." I frowned. Things were getting increasingly difficult, and the Moon Ritual was over before it barely began. Unfortunately, we would have to go on with the tracking spell. A light breeze blew and ruffled the leaves in the trees, and I shivered, not liking the feeling of foreboding that the wind carried.

"I will have to leave my family," I said, coming up with the best plan. "Someone will have to wipe their memories," I said, looking at each of them in turn. "And then we will have to leave this town. Our mark is all over it, I'm surprised the owner of the mind probe hasn't found us yet."

"It is not *us* that it was after," Alpheus said quietly, and at first I didn't understand why he sounded so dismayed. "It was *you*."

My mind was made up in seconds.

"Alpheus, wipe my parents' minds, I was never born. Gwenwyn follow Alpheus and pack my things. Everyone else pack everything you need, we have to leave as soon as possible. Quinteth, pack Gwenwyn's things for her as well. I will wipe the townsfolk's minds."

I dismissed them by running directly to the tower. I raced as fast as I could towards the top floor. I quickly drew my pentagram, and put the thick white candles all around the drawing. "*Light!*" I ordered and power seeped out through my hands to flow to the candles and they lighted up with my signature purple flames.

"May the powers of nature side with me," I prayed quickly. "*Initiate mind-wipe.*"

The candles started swirling around me, lifting off the ground. I waited for the words of power to fill my mind. My head blanked out, all thoughts disappearing.

"*Hidden truths for obvious lies, heightened, crept into the minds, scouring searchless left unseen, truths defy for lies untie.*" I raised my hands and chanted the incantation loudly. Clouds of thunder rolled across the night sky and my body shuddered from the cold. Rain started pelting down on the ground.

"*Release!*" I cried, and all the power that had been building in me exploded outwards. I felt a great wave of energy blast out through the walls of the tower, and I focused on the things I wanted the townsfolk to forget. I felt all the minds of the townsfolk in my own, and willed them to forget about me, about the Bloods, and about their very own past. Their minds would forget the memories I wanted them to, and create their own to replace the holes.

I was careful to watch out for my friends' minds so that I didn't accidentally wipe them as well. I was also careful to watch out for anymore mind probes as well, promising to wipe the probe so cleanly that the dark mage would forget its own name.

Then the winds died down, and I knew it was over, and the candles flew back to the places they were originally at before the spell. I felt tired, but not drained. My power regenerated very quickly, so I would be back to full health with a full might's rest.

I saw the two big bags that my friends had used to carry the spell ingredients to the tower. The bags were empty, but I rectified it quickly, filling them up with all the things we needed and was glad that everything could fit. Then I sat down on the small stool in the corner, trying to figure out why everything that was happening happened.

Was it something I did? Someone I had spited? I never spited anyone if I could help it, so it couldn't be that. Perhaps it all came down to the most basic of things about having power. To be a white mage, there has to be dark mages to contrast, otherwise we would all just be mages. It was another power paradox.

To have me gone, it would mean the dark mages were up to something big. It was something that only I could stop, but why haven't they already done it in my absence? My frown deepened. Why haven't they done it yet? My mind was reeling with the confusion.

Just as something terrifying dawned on me, I sensed a few people coming towards the tower. It was my friends. I grabbed the bags, and struggled with it down the steps. Alpheus met me halfway, and he took both bags off of me. We walked on in silence. I didn't have to ask to know that the mind wipe of my parents had gone well. It was Alpheus after all.

My parents needed to be wiped separately and directly, because they were directly related to me, and because I was of their blood, they wouldn't really be affected by me, so Alpheus had to do it. The amount of power paradoxes today were suffocating.

In the silence, just being next to this beautiful boy kept me sane. His sweet, calming presence soothed the turmoil in my heart and mind. I think the reason why I kept calling him beautiful was because he had always felt beautiful to me. His mere presence was really . . . beautiful. Yeah, that was the only word for it.

He looked at me tranquilly. "I have a car. We will be at the next town by daybreak."

We got out of the tower, and I breathed in the cold air. The ground was wet from the rain.

"We will get to the bottom of this," I swore. I felt my parents' numbed minds. And then I will come back to be your Wendy.

Chapter 9

BACK TO SQUARE ONE

"We should go to Settleburg City first, because I was born there. There are minds to be wiped and . . . and . . ." I didn't know how to say this, but I had to break up with Mark in person. I owed him that much after swearing that he would never lose me. Especially since I was going to mind wipe all his memories of me after that. My fingers automatically touched the necklace that he gave me. I had yet to take it off.

"And what, Crescentia?" Gwenwyn asked from where she sat in the backseat, with Quinteth on her left, and Ezra on her right.

"And . . ." yeah, there was really no way for me to say this. I sneaked a look at Alpheus who was driving. He didn't seem particularly concerned, but that was because I was Shielding my mind so that he couldn't read my thoughts.

The jeep jerked slightly over a bump. Yeah, when Alpheus said *car*, I hadn't realised that he meant *jeep*, and frankly, I was glad of it. There was a lot more space in the jeep to be comfy. I was sitting in the shotgun seat.

"And I have to . . . uh . . . let someone down," I said uncomfortably. It was the only way of telling the truth without actually saying it. I'd turned my phone off so that the others wouldn't know what was truly going on, which was that I had more than twenty missed calls from Mark. I just couldn't bear to speak to him after knowing Alpheus again.

"Let someone down . . . ?" Ezra muttered, and I could feel their thoughts forming around that phone call I'd picked up in the garden. They must have been thinking about it pretty loudly, because Alpheus understood. And I knew he understood because his hands tightened on the wheel slightly. Yikes.

I didn't know what to say after that, because there were two types of silences in the jeep. The first type came from my friends' guilty pleasure in the interesting events that may or may not unfold. The second came from a particularly stony Alpheus.

Yikes, again. I decided that the best course of action would be to go to sleep to regain strength, because there was nothing I could do about either silences.

I woke up about three hours later when Alpheus stopped the jeep at the next town's petrol station to refill the tank. We'd left Queenstown with only a quarter tank, so he wanted to make it full before we continued on our way to Settleburg City.

He got out and went to the store to pay first, and the rest of us got out to stretch our legs. I jogged on the spot for two seconds, and slid back into the jeep. I watched the three of them discuss buying snacks as they went in. I watched them debate over which snacks to choose and I rolled my eyes.

They would end up listening to Gwenwyn, so I didn't know why they ever bothered. Then my attention was diverted to a certain beautiful individual coming out of the store to pump the fuel into the tank. I got out and silently stood beside him.

Are you angry?

There was no response. He wasn't shutting me out; he just didn't know what to say.

Please don't be mad at me, I begged.

This time, I had incited a sigh from him. He looked at me tenderly.

"How can I be mad at you?" he said softly. His thoughts swirled around the jealousy he was feeling. "It doesn't make any sense, but it hurts."

I swallowed. I hurt him again. And this pain hurt me, just like the one before. We were one and the same.

"It's different, Alpheus," I said. "He is a childhood playmate, nothing more."

He nodded. He knew I meant it; he just needed time to wrap his head around this. He hadn't felt jealousy in a long time. He hadn't felt it in more than a millennium. I put my hand on his arms gently, gratified that he didn't pull away. I let my love for him flow through our contact, so that he knew what he meant to me.

He leaned back and closed his eyes, a small smile on his face. The pump popped and he opened his eyes, taking it out and putting it back in the stand. Then he looked at me, and there was humour in his expression.

"Do you know that we've really just met two days ago?" he said, wrapping his arms around me, his breathtaking eyes twinkling like stars with amusement. "You should not be swayed so easily by strangers."

I laughed softly in his arms. "You, a stranger? I don't think that's possible."

I tightened my hold on him and raised myself on my toes, and he pressed his lips to mine. Then his hands held my waist and lifted me against him and we kissed hard.

I felt like I was giving my life over to him, and the notion thrilled me to no end. I wound my fingers in his soft angel hair and pulled him closer to me. He lifted me higher and I wrapped my legs around his waist, and he pressed my back against the jeep. We were pressed up to each other in wanton need.

I pulled my head back for air, and he moved his lips down my neck. I shivered deliciously when he nipped my collarbone. I tilted my head back to enjoy this feeling. This was the stuff that dreams were made of. When I pulled his face back up to kiss him, there was an intense look of hunger in his silvery grey eyes that made my breath catch and my heartbeat speed up.

I purposely held him in place as I slowly touched my lips to his. His mouth opened slightly and I pressed the tip of my tongue to his bottom lip. He kept one hand on my waist, and the other came up to my hair and he pulled me in. He slipped his tongue into my mouth and I pressed my own against it. I felt like I was going to combust with the feelings that he put me through. I wanted him so badly. I could tell he wanted me, too, with the way he was pressing against me.

"Our teeth are gonna rot." I heard Ezra complain at Gwenwyn as they came out of the store, and I was disappointed when Alpheus slowly stepped away from me and put me down again. I hugged him one more time, and he kissed the top of my head.

"I have deemed it necessary according to our travelling time's uncertainty," Gwenwyn declared in an important voice. "At the very least, we won't be buying anymore for the next few weeks."

"The next few *months,*" Quinteth corrected.

"It doesn't really matter; Gwenwyn would be able to finish it all by herself in one day," Ezra muttered grumpily.

We walked over to the front of the jeep, and I smiled giddily at what almost happened. Alpheus nodded at them, taking all the jostling at face value and went into the jeep.

"Next stop, Settleburg City," Alpheus announced, and off we went.

Somewhere between three songs and a packet of potato chips, I'd fallen asleep again. I was woken up this time by someone nudging me awake.

"Crescentia, please wake up." I heard Alpheus's beautiful voice calling me back from the edge of sleep.

"Hurm . . . ?" I murmured, knuckling the sleep from my eyes. I knuckled my own eyes a bit too hard and saw stars. I had to stop doing that or I'd go blind.

"Do you know any convenient inns in the city?" Alpheus asked me. The question made me bolt into an upright position.

I looked around and noticed a few familiar places. "Ah, turn left right here, then you'll see a stretch of foreign restaurants and then at the corner, turn in left again."

Alpheus followed my directions and turned.

"There, you see that? It's an inn."

"That looks more like a hotel than an inn," Ezra mumbled, his voice thick with sleep, looking out the window for the first time. "Can we afford that?"

"Well, that's what city inns look like," I said smugly. "You can park inside; they only allow parking for customers," I told Alpheus.

The large sign on the outside of the inn said: "Holiday Inn". I watched as Alpheus navigates his way expertly through the inn's car park. You'd have thought he went out driving in inns parking space every day the way he did it so well. Once he was parked, an attendant came out to welcome us, and we were ushered in. The building was five storeys high.

The attendant babbled stuff about us enjoying our time at the pool, or relaxing at the spa, or whatever else that we didn't listen to. Alpheus took charge and didn't waste any time by straightaway checking in, and we carried our luggage up the lift.

We didn't bring all our stuff, just the ingredients we needed for the mind-wiping spell, and a few backups—just in case—and enough clothes for the day. We also brought ingredients for the tracking spell, since we never actually managed to perform the tracking spell back in Queenstown.

The boys had their own room and the girls had our own room. I'd wanted to share a room with Alpheus, but we both knew we had to watch our funds. Once we were settled in, I let the other two girls chill, and I went to the balcony, locked it from the outside and finally turned on my phone. I read the notices and saw that I had another twelve missed calls in addition to the first twenty.

I dialled Mark's number and waited. I didn't have to wait long, because he picked up on the first ring.

"Wendy, baby!" he breathed. "You freaking worried me. I called you and you were always unreachable. Did your battery die or something?"

I found it hard to reply. This was Mark, the guy who been through all my weird moods and tantrums and put up with me, even falling in love with me. This was the same Mark who had given me the necklace that I still wore around my neck as proof of us being together.

It wasn't that I didn't love him anymore; it was just that I'd discovered that my love for him was friendlier than true love, as I knew it was with Alpheus.

"Wendy?" Mark called when I didn't respond.

"Uh, yeah, hey, I'm actually in town now," I said quickly. "Would you like to meet up? There's something important that I have to tell you."

"Oh, man, that's great!" Mark said enthusiastically. "When and where?"

"How about the Pavilion, at three p.m.?" I suggested. It was barely noon now, I had plenty of time to shower and relax first, and tell my friends what I intended to do.

The Pavilion was one of the largest shopping malls in the city. It was more of a megamall.

"Okay, sure. Did you come with your parents?" He asked. I bit my lip. That was a hard question to answer truthfully. My parents don't remember me anymore. I held back the hurt that that thought brought upon me.

"Look, Mark, I've got to go. See you soon." I quickly hung up and closed my eyes, letting the guilt ride through my mind. I flashed back to the day my parents told me that I was moving to Queenstown, when Mark had truly kissed me for the first time.

"Never," I'd sworn. I had given him my oath that he would never lose me, and after just two weeks plus at a different town, I was throwing my word out the window. It was definitely not the most normal of circumstances, but still, I felt guilty for it anyway. The thought of giving up Alpheus never even crossed my mind. That was an impossible feat.

I heaved a very heavy sigh and went back into the room where I showered, and rested for an hour. Then when I woke up feeling refreshed, we went down to the restaurants at the opposite side of the road. I brought the ingredients for the mind wiping and tracking spell.

"I'll order," I offered, seeing frown after frown descend upon their faces as they studied the menu. I ordered a five course seafood meal. I hoped that would suffice for Gwenwyn.

"Uh guys? I have something to tell you," I started, ignoring the nerves. "We have to wipe the minds of this town out so that none of them remember me. I will need your help on this, because—" whatever I was about to say cut off when a waiter came to put our settings down and left. "—because the city is about six times bigger than Queenstown," I continued. "I will be meeting a few of my friends at the Pavilion at three, which is in two hours, to end things properly before I wipe their minds."

"We will perform the Ritual from the top of the Pavilion, because it is eighty floors high, which will give us some good leverage," I told them, and they nodded, acknowledging my plans. The first course came and we worked our way through to the fifth course. We were all stuffed except for Gwenwyn, even though she ate more than all of us added together.

I looked at the clock on the wall and saw that it was already two forty, so I called for the bill and paid, and we quickly left. We took Alpheus's jeep and I directed the way through the busy streets of Settleburg. They were quite awed at the skyscrapers and tall office buildings, down to the opera houses and theatres.

"Yeah, it's that one," I said, pointing to the humongous megamall. Tourists and shoppers filled the roads, and shopping bags covered them from head to toe. It caused a major traffic jam, so we parked away from the mall and walked. I was going to be late, but that was alright, because I—as Wendy—was always late to any meeting I had anyway.

I told them to take the lift to the roof, and make sure that there was no one around, and mesmerise some security guards to make it a "no access" place for people other than us.

As we walked into the mall, I started walking away from them towards the place I'd promised to meet Mark. I turned back to give them one last instruction.

"Remember; wait until I give the signal," I warned, and then I took off. I tried to calm my breathing on the escalator all the way to the third floor. I saw Mark there, standing outside the Pizza Hut franchise, waiting for me. He saw me as I came up the escalator, and a warm smile spread across his face. I bit my lip. This was going to be harder than I'd thought.

I walked towards him and motioned for us to sit inside. I ordered a Coke and he had one as well, his eyes never leaving my face.

"What is it?" he murmured. I winced internally. He grew up with me in this life, so of course he was sensitive to my thoughts. He knew something was up.

"I . . . I . . ." I just couldn't start my sentence. How was I going to say this? I met someone I used to be in love with before I died and now that I'm reincarnated I want to be with him again? *Not likely.*

"Come on, Wends, spit it out." He rolled his eyes. "Wends", wow I haven't been called that in a long time. But after today, in a few more hours, actually, I would never be called that again. Was that really what I wanted? I truly didn't want to erase my consciousness as Wendy. I bit my lip, frustrated, feeling my frown deepen.

"Hey, Wendy, come on, babe." He put his hand on mine, and I yanked my hand away, a knee-jerk reaction. I saw hurt enter his eyes as he slowly understood what was going on. "Did you . . . meet someone else?" he said in a voice that he fought to keep steady. When I didn't—couldn't—answer, hurt filled his eyes and he looked away.

"It's different, not quite that I met someone else," I said softly. In all honesty, it should be Mark who was the "someone else". I bit my lip again, feeling it get chapped up.

"Then what is it?" he muttered, mute pain in his voice. My heart squeezed in aching hurt.

"I . . . I was never really in love with you," I explained quietly. "It's more of a friendly love."

He shook his head sharply. "Then you never should have said yes." His words came out harsh and hurt. I looked down at the table.

"I'm sorry, Mark. I really . . ." I trailed off. I didn't know how to end that sentence.

"So, it's not me, it's you, right?" he said, trying to hide his pain by joking, ever the gentleman. He wanted me, but he also wanted me to be happy. If this was my way of being happy, he wasn't going to let me watch him suffer over it. The guilt had weighed on my heart was overwhelming.

"Right," I returned his smile with a small rueful one. I wanted to tell him if that situation was different, we would be together, but it was impossible to say, because Alpheus was always at the back of my mind. "Look, I'm sort of on a trip and I left to talk to you, so I need to get back now," I told him.

He nodded, not saying anything.

I reached over and squeezed his hand. He turned his hand up and caught mine, holding tightly, and I felt all of his pain in that one touch. I almost cried out from the shock of it. Then he released me.

"You should probably call Remora. She won't stop worrying about you." He muttered and pointed to my necklace. "You don't have to force yourself to wear that."

"I will always wear this." I breathed helplessly. It was selfish of me, but I couldn't help it. I wished I wasn't a witch so that I couldn't feel other people's emotions.

I looked at him, but he had turned to stone, staring at the table. I turned and left quickly. I knew he wouldn't want me to watch him fall apart. I took out my phone and dialled Alpheus's number.

He picked up on the first ring. "Is it time?" his calm voice asked. I nodded, choked up. I was surprised to feel tears running down my face. Then I realised that he couldn't see me nod.

"Yes, put everything in place," I whispered brokenly. The other side of the line was silent for a moment.

"Okay," he said. He didn't hang up, but left the line open so that I could feel his presence. I was grateful for that. There was nothing he could say that could change the way I was feeling, so he did what he always did. He just stayed there for me. Only Alpheus could have come up with such an uncompromising solution.

I heard them move the preparations around until it reached their satisfaction level. I got off the escalator at the roof and closed the phone. It was showtime.

We finished the mind wiping spell quickly and set the place for the tracking spell. Once the candles were set in a tight triangle around us, I picked up the vial of blood and drew the tracking spell pentagram, not my own. This was more serious than the time needed. I drew pentagrams quickly anyway. The vial was a magically enchanted one that was handed to me by Mordent, my original mother. I only had to put a drop of my blood and it would keep filling up infinitely.

I closed my eyes and raised my hands. My friends stood around me at square points. This time, words were not needed. The candles lighted up by themselves, the power in the air was charged and heavy.

The spell formed by itself, absorbing the materials in the pentagram at my feet. Then a massive wind picked up inside the pentagram, coming from the ground below my feet, where the pentagram was drawn. The wind blew upwards, my hair flying up with it.

My friends kept their eyes closed, chanting the words of the spell. Only they had to say it, I didn't.

"Lost be found, dark be light." They chanted over and over.

I brought my mind back to the time when we were having our Moon Ritual, the time I had sensed the mind probe. I grasped onto the feel of the mind probe, containing the feel and throwing it out through my hands into the magical wind. The wind roared and the sound blasted in my ears.

I stood there firmly, my face raised towards to sky. I felt the power in me flow out through my hands, and pour into the wind. The spell pulled on my power, going further and further throughout the Regions. There were traces of the same presence all around, but there was nothing concrete.

The spell expanded out of Settleburg City, moving on through North Hunter's Woods, then Royal City, and then South Hunter's Woods, and then finally slowed down at Rigs City. The presence was very prominently there, and I pushed the spell forward, starting to feel slightly drained, trying to pinpoint the spot exactly. It was in a small district in Rigs City. There was a very dark aura about the entire district in that city. What was worse was that I started to recognise the presence.

I contained the presence in my mind, making sure that it was traceable, and slowly stopped the flow of power to the tracking spell. Now I would know whenever and wherever the dark presence moved. The spell ended as suddenly as it began. The flow of magic stopped and the wind cut off abruptly.

"It is finished. Thank you," I murmured. I was thanking the power all around me and in me, and also the power of nature. If I didn't, I wasn't sure what would happen next time. I opened my eyes and lowered my hands. My friends had stopped chanting once the spell had stopped, and they were down on one knee, their way of thanks to the powers. They weren't as graced in the powers as I was, so their thanks had to be more pronounced.

I stepped out of the pentagram and looked at them. "It is in Rigs City. We must adjourn there."

They frowned, and I knew why. Rigs City was the southernmost part of the Regions, and also the most dangerous. It wasn't really surprising, in a sense that the dark mages would be attracted to that place. It was also very far away, perhaps a three week journey, even with the jeep.

"It's time to go." Alpheus said, and we started clearing up.

We packed up everything and cleared the pentagram off the ground, and I watched as they thanked the mesmerised security guard who ushered us out like VIPs.

"I'd do anything for you guys, anytime," he said with an unfocused, dazed expression on his face. I chuckled. They may have used a bit too much power, but the great thing about the *Mesmer* was that there were no side effects, and once the mesmerised people recovered, they wouldn't remember a thing that they were mesmerised to do.

We reached the inn by evening due to the excruciatingly long traffic jams, and we all agreed to hit the sack early.

Chapter 10

MANY UNUSUAL INCIDENTS

When I opened my eyes for the third time since we started our journey away from Queenstown, I was greeted with the most brilliant hues of red-gold light. It was the sunrise at its best peak.

I got off the inn bed, careful not to wake Gwenwyn and Quinteth, and walked towards the balcony as if in a daze. I opened the door that led to the balcony and then stepped out, closing my eyes to feel the rays of light on my face.

It was a controlled, sweet power, but I wasn't interested in harvesting the power just yet. I just wanted to feel the gentle light smooth my worries away, and wash them from my mind. I smiled unconsciously.

It is so beautiful, I couldn't help thinking.

It is, isn't it?

I heard Alpheus's voice flow into my mind and I guessed that he was seeing the same thing that I was. I turned to the right just in time to watch Alpheus step out of his room, and onto his balcony. He looked incredibly hot with a natural bed head of pale golden hair and casual t-shirt and sweat pants. I knew he was checking me out as well.

We smiled at each other, and simultaneously turned to continue watching the sunrise. I could feel us getting connected even with all the space between us, and the air crackled with electricity. I looked at him to see that he was looking at me, too. We simultaneously walked towards the end of our balconies and I was thrilled to find that we were within touching distance.

We held each other close, occasionally slipping in a kiss or two for a few more moments until the sun climbed away from the perfect height, and became too bright for our eyes. As we re-entered our room to our friends who were all just starting to wake, I couldn't forget the awe I had felt at watching the view; the rays had made all the buildings look like they had been caught on fire.

After packing our meagre belongings from the rooms at the inn, Alpheus checked us out at noon and we had late brunch at a restaurant opposite the inn. It was a different one than the one we ate at the day before. Then we were off, back on the road.

After just two hours on the road, we became aware that we were forgetting something important for a long term drive: proper food. Sure, Gwenwyn had bought out the snack bar with a motherload, but those were ultimately just snacks; junk food that wouldn't give our bodies the nutrition it needed.

Also, Gwenwyn had unsurprisingly developed a stomach-ache from continuously eating the incredibly unhealthy junk food. Hey, I'm not knocking junk food. I love me some chips and dip, but watching Gwenwyn shovel sweets and other junk into her face made my stomach turn.

I could tell by looking in the rearview mirror that Quinteth and Ezra had been uncomfortable as well, as they studiously stared hard out the windows, trying to ignore the sounds of her crunching. I remembered wondering if Quinteth and Ezra were dating, and I realised that they may actually have feelings for each other.

"When is the next stop?" Gwenwyn gasped for the sixth time since the time she got sick, which was exactly twenty minutes ago.

"In the next town," Ezra and Quinteth said in perfect unison. The difference between their words was the tone they had used. Ezra's tone contained muted impatience while Quinteth's tone contained muted concern. Alpheus's brow twitched.

They have been very close to each other these few centuries, he informed me in amusement.

I stifled a laugh and it came out muffled. It was very cruel of me to be amused at my friends' discomfort, but I couldn't help it. I hoped that Gwenwyn would learn a lesson from this, but she most likely wouldn't, so I was enjoying watching her face the consequences of her bad choice while it lasted. I sounded quite the sadist.

Of course, I was worried as well, but not as worried as I would have been if I hadn't been Wendy. I'd gotten sick plenty of times as a child when my parents let me indulge too thoroughly in sweets.

"Just close your eyes and press your cheek on the window frame,' I repeated my advice to her. "The wind will help."

I'd gotten her to switch places with Quinteth so that she could lean her head against the window frame to let the wind blow against her face. It had helped a little after a while; she had stopped looking green.

I leaned back in my seat as well, enjoying the feel of the wind on my face. I had had to tie my long hair up because it had whipped Alpheus in the face and caused him to swerve on the road. There were still some tiny hair marks on one side of his face to show for it. It must have hurt, but he didn't say anything.

All our windows were down because the air conditioning was pointless with Gwenwyn's window down. The incident of my hair whipping had made both Gwenwyn and Quinteth tie up their hair as well, not wanting to hurt anybody.

Once Ezra had finished laughing at the hair-in-Alpheus's-face incident, he had referred to it as "death by hair", which made us crack up and imagine weird stuff.

As we passed the many wide plantation fields that decorated the side of the road, we slowly noticed that there were more huts and houses popping up, which was the cue for the next town. Sure enough, before ten minutes were out, we were zipping past a large road sign that read: "Welcome to Wilkinson Town".

"Wilkinson Town is a metal town, I think," I said, frowning, trying to focus on my thoughts. I'd never been out of Settleburg before, save one school trip to Royal City, but we didn't have any pit stops because we went in caravans, so we were pretty much self-sustained. "They are also a trading town. I think they trade with America, a few countries in the Europe and Malaysia, but I'm not sure."

"What does a metal town mean?" Quinteth asked.

"It doesn't matter right now!" Gwenwyn gasped. "*Please* get me to the nearest rest house!" The green shade had slipped under her skin again.

Alpheus nodded, searching for a rest house with his eyes.

"It's time like this when our powers would come in handy," Ezra grumbled.

I frowned. "No, Ezra. You know the rules. Our magic is only to help others, never ourselves."

They nodded and shared a common expression, and I knew it was because they'd heard the same line so many times before. I suppressed a smile. Gwenwyn groaned and Alpheus frowned, his steady calm shaken. He didn't like being unable to do something while someone else was in pain.

Finally, we all spotted a gas station, the kind with a mini mart and toilets. Alpheus more or less flew the last few metres towards the station and Gwenwyn more or less flew out of the jeep and into the ladies. I chuckled at their antics.

Quinteth and Ezra got out and stretched their legs. I got out to stretch my legs as well and looked around. The sky in Wilkinson Town was murky and grey and the air smelled quite stale. It didn't take long to figure out why.

"I was right, it is a metal town," I muttered, looking at the factories that rose from the ground around us. The black smoke huffed and puffed in huge clouds into the sky.

"That's right; you didn't tell us what a metal town is," Quinteth reminded me. Alpheus got out and ran a check on the jeep.

"It's a manufacturing town." I wasn't surprised that they knew so little about the world even though they had never left it. That was because they had never left Queenstown as well. "This town produces vehicles, weapons, gifts, anything made from metal," I explained. "That's because—"

"—because we have metal ore," A deep voice said.

We all turned to the left, where a group of youngsters were walking up to us. There were two boys and one girl, and all of them were slightly on the buff side. All three of them looked us up and down. I didn't like the way the girl's eyes latched onto Alpheus. It was obvious that she thought he was beautiful, too. I mean, who wouldn't?

I stepped forward. "Hey, guys. I'm Wendy, and these are my friends, Summer, Jason and Corey. Snowy is in the washroom, so you'll see her later."

The one of the guys, the blond one, stepped forward. "I'm Keith and this is Jillian and Tom." We all nodded awkwardly at each other. "So what brings you lovely folk to this town?" Keith drawled.

"I'm going to buy a litre," Alpheus told me, ignoring everybody else, and turned to go into the mini mart. He didn't like talking to strangers. It had something to do with where he came from.

"A litre of what?" The girl asked, confusion swept across her face.

"Probably oil. We're on a backpacking trip," I explained. Quinteth and Ezra were wearing their stranger-friendly smiles, and their good looks were not lost on the other side.

Tom stared at me. "You guys don't have school to go to?"

I shrugged. "We're dropouts."

The three of them seemed to think this was funny and they sniggered. "Well, how about we show you another side of our town; the unpolluted side." Keith smiled with genuine warmth and I responded with a smile as well. I didn't let my guards down, though. I didn't like the way they looked at us, as if they were hungry for entertainment.

Alpheus came out of the shop carrying a can of fuel that was a litre full but the way he carried it made it look like it was empty. He went straight to the car and popped the boot. I realised we were all staring at him because he carried his nonchalant air about him.

"Corey, what do you think?" I asked him. He looked up thoughtfully while his hands found space to put the can without letting it come into contact with our bags.

"We need to replenish healthy food supplies," he said. We all thought about poor Gwenwyn and agreed.

"I will go check up on Snowy," Quinteth said, and left us. Now that I was the only girl there, Jillian sized me up. I wanted to shrink back, but something told me that wouldn't be a good idea.

"There's a grocery store at the other side of town. Tourists always come through this way and they instantly don't like it here, but they haven't got the chance to see the sweet side of this town," Keith said. I noticed that they were all dressed in khakis.

"Okay, once Snowy is alright, we'll go," Ezra said, effectively ending proper conversation.

"Do you want us to wait with you?" Keith asked. He had dark, bushy eyebrows and sparkling sea-green eyes. It was a very interesting contrast. "It's our off day today, so we're free."

I shook my head. "It's cool; you guys go on ahead first." I slipped into Wendy's slang easily.

They nodded and waved goodbye to us after telling me some directions. I paced the area around the jeep while waiting for Gwenwyn. Ezra watched me for a while and then decided to make better use of his time by going to sleep in the jeep. I approved of that because we needed all the rest we could get, but I couldn't seem to stop my pacing.

Alpheus watched me for a few minutes more before putting a hand on my shoulder. He pulled me in and I hugged him, breathing in his sweet scent and my head cleared a bit. I admit I was getting a bit edgy from the terrible pollution.

He kissed the top of my head, letting his calm flow over to me. I accepted it, melting into his arms. As naughty thoughts of what I wanted to do with Alpheus just entered my head, Gwenwyn's voice ruined the moment.

"Oh, man, I feel so much better now!" Gwenwyn's happy voice reached to my ears and we all got up and turned to face her. She looked slightly dishevelled but Quinteth poked her hair here and there and she looked normal again. "Can I get a breath mint?"

We all laughed and waited as she and Quinteth went into the mini mart. A few people who looked like tourists came out and nodded towards us and left in their automobile.

Once they were out, we settled into the jeep once more, but this time our windows were up. I remembered the directions given by Keith and told Alpheus. It was an amazing thing to watch as the ugly factories slowly turned into a proper rural town with motor workshops and coffee shops and other shops. The streets were paved with stone and somehow it was all quite nice to look at.

We tried searching for the grocery store that Keith had mentioned but it was hard because there were many market-like places as well. Then suddenly we saw the three of them on one side of the street, waving to us. I waved back and Alpheus followed them. Finally we broke through the crowds and found the grocery store. All of us couldn't help staring. It looked like a Tesco.

We all got out and waited for the three Wilkinson Town teens to reach the store. We could see them navigating their way through. Then we faced each other and their eyes fell on Gwenwyn, firstly because they haven't seen her, and secondly because they'd probably never seen anyone like her before.

Everyone in this town were all on the burly side, even the kids, so seeing someone as small as Gwenwyn was probably something of a cultural shock to them. They couldn't take their eyes off of her.

"This is Snowy," I introduced, and she stepped forward in her slightly arrogant manner—like a grandmother—and held out her hand to shake. "Snowy, this is Keith, Jillian and Tom."

They took turns shaking her hand, marvelling at the smoothness of her skin. She withdrew quickly and stepped behind me.

"Let's go in," I suggested. We all started going into the store. We were hit by the smell of baking bread as soon as we stepped in. There was a small bakery inside.

"I'll go get some buns. Summer and Jason, you guys go buy some canned food," I said. Gwenwyn looked at me expectantly, waiting for her orders. I just shrugged.

"You can do whatever you want, I guess, except buy food." Everyone laughed at this. She turned bright red and looked at the floor. I felt bad instantly, and hugged her. "I'm kidding. You can choose some dehydrated food and get the water."

"We'll go with, uh, Snowy," Keith said. We watched as the three of them follow Gwenwyn like overgrown puppies. They looked like they were asking a lot of questions and Gwenwyn looked like she was seriously answering them.

We looked at each other and chuckled. Quinteth motioned Ezra to go and they went hunting for the canned food. I turned into the bakery, holding hands with Alpheus. We looked at the many assorted types of bread there were on the shelves.

"This one, definitely," I quipped, using the clippers and putting the chocolate covered bun on my tray. Alpheus smiled, watching me enjoy myself choosing the bread.

"What about this one?" he asked, pointing.

"Oh, that looks good," I replied, clipping that up, too.

We kept that up until our tray was full and went over to the counter. Some of the townsfolk had watched at us unashamedly, clearly amused to see us debate over bread.

"Hello, there," The cashier at the counter said amiably. He looked withered and old but also neat and clean. "I've never seen you two lovely youngsters before. Where do you hail from?"

We looked at each other and smiled. It was probably obvious that we were together.

"I'm from Settleburg City, and he's from Queenstown," I said, smiling. Alpheus took out his wallet while the old man rang up the bread. I wondered if I should have said that, because we had already wiped all our traces from the two places. It didn't matter, because it would have been the same if I'd said some other place that I haven't been.

"Ah, so you're a city girl, then?" The old man chuckled. "We don't get many of those around here. I've been to Settleburg once. It was an amazing place." He set the bread in a paper bag on the counter. "It's ten dollars and twenty cents."

Alpheus handed over the cash and said thanks and took the bag.

"Oh, before I forget, since today is the third of June, there's a festival tonight. It's called the Politer Festival," The old man said. "That's when we all dress up as people of the eighteenth century, when the metals works have started to bloom. There are moving floats and all that."

I was intrigued. "Really? That sounds so cool." I turned to Alpheus. "Doesn't it?"

He shrugged. "I suppose so. But we cannot stay for it."

I remembered our task and the only reason we even stopped here was to buy food, and let Gwenwyn use the loo. "Oh, that's right. Well, that's okay then."

We waved goodbye to him, and walked out of the bakery.

"Do you want to look for them or just walk around?" I asked Alpheus. I held his hand—the one that wasn't carrying the paper bag. He kissed my fingertips, and a tingling sensation spread throughout my body.

"Well . . ." but before he could give me an answer, Quinteth and Ezra came around the corner and walked towards us, waving a paper bag of canned food.

Just so you know, I would have said 'walk around'.

I looked at him and smiled, rolling my eyes.

"Isn't Gwenwyn here yet?" Ezra asked.

She came around a different corner, chatting amiably with the three Wilkinson Town kids.

"Speak of the devil," I said. "And the devil shall appear."

She was close enough to hear me and she frowned. "I'm not a devil," She protested.

"It's just a saying." I grinned at her.

"So, there's this festival tonight," Keith cut in.

"The Politer Festival, right?" I said, remembering.

The three Wilkinson Town kids looked surprised. "How did you know about it?" Jillian asked, grudgingly amazed.

"The cashier told us," Alpheus said serenely. Jillian's eyes latched on to him. I frowned.

"Oh yeah, that's old man Cyrus. So will you guys be coming?" I was absolutely sure that the last sentence was directed at Gwenwyn. Tom looked at her expectantly, and she looked at me expectantly.

I shook my head. "We would really like to, but we're kinda on a tight schedule."

Jillian stepped forward, scowling. "Hey, what's your problem? Do you own them or something? Why do they have to listen to you?"

I took a step back, shocked. "What?"

Alpheus took a step so that he stood in front of me. Quinteth stood on my left and Ezra stood on my right. All three of them stared them down.

"Every time I hear you open your mouth, you're ordering them around like they're your servants," Jillian snapped and shoved away Tom's restraining hands.

Gwenwyn stood right up to Jillian and shocked us all by slapping her across the face. Jillian glared at her angrily.

"She's more than you think," Gwenwyn said steely. "Nobody is allowed to insult her, ever."

"That's enough, Snowy, let's go in peace," I said quickly, and realised that Jillian was right. Every time I opened my mouth, I was telling them what to do.

"Again!" Jillian yelled. A lot of people were looking now. Keith stepped forward and bodily restrained her back.

"Sorry, she's sensitive. She hates authorities of all sorts." He said quickly. "But hey, I like a girl who can command." He winked at me.

Alpheus's mouth pressed into a thin line.

"Uh, yeah, okay," I said, pulling on their shirts. "Let's go." We moved quickly out of the store and into the car park while Tom and Keith held Jillian back. She continued to yell curses after me.

I was quiet as we drove out of town and onto the highway. Alpheus put his hand on my knee.

"Come on, Crescentia, stop sulking," Ezra muttered. "You're bringing our mood down. That was really funny wasn't it?" his chuckle withered in his throat when he saw the look that Alpheus levelled at him in the rearview mirror.

"Am I really that bad?" I whispered, not liking the truth about me.

"If you don't command us, then someone else will, and we would really rather it be you," Quinteth said.

"When we were Bound, we gave our oath, remember?" Gwenwyn said. I thought about their words and was much relieved. Quinteth's words especially made me feel better.

"Okay," I said with a small smile.

Chapter 11

ON THE ROAD

We started a singing marathon after five boring hours on the road. I played the songs on my phone and we sang along to it. I was glad that I had charged my battery and my power bank to the max, so I didn't have to worry about my battery going flat for the next three days.

As it approached night, we pulled over on the side of the road and wrapped ourselves in blankets. I put a small cushion over the handbrake so that I could lean comfortably over it to rest my head on Alpheus's chest. He enveloped me in his strong, warm arms and we fell asleep.

A rooster crowed.

I opened my eyes to see that we were already back on the road, and Ezra was driving. Quinteth was in the shotgun seat, sound asleep and holding hands with Ezra. He only used one hand to drive. Gwenwyn was on the other side of the backseat. I was in the middle, between Alpheus and Gwenwyn. Ezra must have moved us. When I turned my head to look, Alpheus tightened his arms around me and

I smiled. I kissed his cheek because it was the only part I could reach without moving.

His eyes slowly fluttered open and I stared as the sun shone through the window, making his brilliant grey eyes look almost silver. My breath caught and I marvelled again at how beautiful he was. His eyes cut towards me and a small smile curved the sides of his lips.

"Good morning," he greeted me.

"Good morning," I replied. He stared into my eyes.

"Now your eyes are hazel," He informed me. I grinned. I shifted so that his legs were apart and I was sitting between them and he enveloped me.

"Is it now?" I grinned at him cheekily. My eyes changed colour according to surroundings. It wasn't magic, but it was quite uncommon. Adrienne had changing eye colour too. As far as I knew, my eyes could change into four different colours: hazel, orange-green, green and dark grey.

Remora once described to me how my orange-green eyes looked. It was like an orange flower blooming from my pupils and then mixing into leafy green irises. From then on, I'd always liked the orange-green eyes the most. Alpheus had named it sunflower eyes in my past life.

"Yes," he said and kissed the top of my head. Gwenwyn yawned and stretched, jostling me to side a bit.

"Oh, sorry Crescentia," She said, groaning. "Ah, I'm so hungry. Can I have some food?"

I searched for the paper bag of bread and passed it to her. She excitedly dug in. The smell of the bread had us all hungry, and we passed some around. Quinteth woke up and reached for one as well.

"This is so good," Gwenwyn murmured happily, biting into her second one. Everyone agreed. It was perfectly delicious.

"Anyone needs toilet breaks?" Ezra asked when he spotted a sign that said that the next R&R was in another ten kilometres. We all said yes and he nodded in acknowledgement.

Ten kilometres later, we saw the small rest house. Ezra turned in and parked the jeep. We got out and folded the blankets up. The time on my phone said it was nine thirty a.m. I grabbed my toothbrush and toothpaste from my travel bag and when to the toilets.

I looked at myself in the mirror and saw a dishevelled mess of black hair and groaned loudly, earning a strange look from a woman who came out from one of the cubicles. When she saw my head, she giggled and handed me a comb from her bag.

"Oh, thanks," I said gratefully. She nodded. I knew then that she was a mute. My power told me. I quickly yanked the comb through the knotted strands of my hair and tried to smooth it all out fast, not wanting to inconvenience her. She started putting on makeup and it looked like she would be there for a while, so I kept running the comb through my incredibly long hair. It had grown past my butt already.

Finally, I managed to calm my lion's mane and handed the comb back to her. She smiled and waved and I waved back, and then she left. I started to brush my teeth. I stared at the necklace around my neck and felt a wave of homesickness. I missed Alex and Adrienne.

Only Alpheus was at the jeep. He was putting his own toothbrush back into his bag when I showed up.

"Where are the others?" I asked. He looked up and took my toothbrush and toothpaste from me.

"They went to look at the shops just to walk for a while," he replied. I leaned against the door of the jeep while he closed the boot. Then he walked over to me and put both hands on the jeep on either side of my face. I tilted my head up to look into his silvery eyes. There was so much soul in there that I felt my heart start thudding erratically.

He slowly put his lips on mine; barely touching, yet my entire being came alive, buzzing with electricity. My mouth opened slightly and he pressed his lips harder to mine. I ran my hands up his chest and he came closer to press himself against me. Our lips moved in perfect sync and before I knew it, my hands were up in his hair and his hands were around my waist, lifting me up.

We kissed as if our lives depended on it.

After a few more minutes, we both broke away at the same time, coming up for air. What I wanted was to drag him into the jeep and just do the deed but it wasn't the best time or place. We pressed our foreheads together and laughed breathily, panting. We stayed that way until our breathing calmed and he kissed my forehead.

I want you too, Alpheus told me, and there was a tight edge to the thought. I grinned.

I wanted to kiss him again, but by that time our friends had returned, so I just hugged him tightly and then released him, walking to the shotgun seat. They all got in and Alpheus took over the driving again.

Gwenwyn started looking for food as soon as the jeep was on the road. I frowned.

"You're gonna finish all our food," Ezra grumbled, voicing all of our thoughts. Quinteth was frowning as well. Alpheus was looking ahead, but I recognised his worried silence.

"I can't help it. There's nothing else to do," Gwenwyn complained right back. I tried to think of something that could distract all of us, like a game. Just then, a black car zoomed past our jeep and an idea popped into my head.

"How about we count cars?" I suggested. "Let's separate colours. I'll look for white cars, Gwenwyn, you look for yellow cars, Quinteth, you look for black cars, and Ezra, you look for blue cars."

Alpheus had a small smile on his face, knowing what was coming next.

"Alpheus, you look for red cars and green cars," I told him. He needed to exercise his multitasking skills.

"What? He has to concentrate on driving," Ezra said. I shook my head.

"This will be fine." It was Alpheus, after all. "The game starts now!" I declared and we looked eagerly out the jeep windows.

Every hour or so, we passed a big bottle of water around because travelling made us thirsty easily. After three hours from our last stop, there was a turning in to the right to another town called Archtown, but we didn't stop there. We started getting hungry after the fourth hour and opened the canned food.

Thankfully, Gwenwyn had thought to buy plastic disposable spoons, so we could eat right out of the can. I chose a tuna flake can, a beef stew can and a peach can and shared it all with Alpheus. I fed him while he drove so that we wouldn't have to stop.

Once we were satisfied, we bundled all the empty cans into a plastic bag and kept it to throw at our next stop. We passed the sign that said the next R&R was in fifty metres and we went back to our funny little car game.

Alpheus turned in to the next rest house. It was slightly bigger than the one before. There was a fast food restaurant and a mini playground. I carried out the plastic bag and walked with Alpheus to the trash can that was in front of the toilets. I dumped it and went in the wash my hands.

When I came out, Alpheus was there, waiting for me. I smiled at him. We walked over to the playground and sat all around. I sat on the see-saw with Alpheus on the opposite end and Ezra sat on the slide. Quinteth and Gwenwyn sat on another see-saw.

"So," I started. "I counted twenty three white cars."

"I counted twenty seven black cars," Quinteth said a tad smugly.

"I counted only thirteen blue cars," Ezra groaned. He was never one who liked losing. "Hey, Quinteth, switch with me," he pleaded. She just grinned.

"I counted nine yellow cars." Gwenwyn sighed. She moved so that she was bouncing up and down on the see-saw. Quinteth played along.

"There were six red cars and four green ones," Alpheus said. The others looked at him doubtfully, but I believed him. This was a piece of cake for someone like Alpheus.

We looked at each other in silence for a moment, and then burst out laughing. We were on a dangerous mission but here we were, counting the cars we passed based on their colours. It was getting close to sunset now, and the set of people at the rest house changed.

The playground was set ablaze with the amazing rays of sunset. It was almost like sunrise, but everything was in a darker shade. A cool breeze blew and I shivered. It was time to move on.

For the next seven days, our routine was almost the same; travelling in the jeep, creating different games, switching drivers, resting at rest houses. We went in Minuetown once, when we all agreed on sleeping at an inn and having proper showers.

After two weeks, we were nearing Royal City. It was the biggest city in the Regions. There was even a monarchy there that ruled the city, and they had three different currencies because it was so large. More importantly, it marked the ending of our journey. The journey from Royal City to Rigs City was only three days long.

We watched in excitement as we passed the signboard that said Royal City was in the next hundred metres. Gwenwyn munched on the last of our food. It wasn't the food that we'd bought in Wilkinson Town; that food finished a week ago. It was the food that we'd stocked up on in Minuetown.

By all the laws of nature in the world, the amount that we'd bought should have lasted us for a bit more than two weeks, but Gwenwyn had managed to defy the laws of nature by consuming half of it within four days. It was insane.

"Where does it all go, Gwenwyn?" I exclaimed, exasperated. She burped and excused herself.

"It goes to the black hole in my stomach," she replied, and we all laughed at that.

"Hey, that was a good one," Ezra complimented. She grinned, accepting the compliment gracefully.

"Oh, my, you guys, look!" Quinteth suddenly called out. The view that graced our eyes was magnificent.

We scrolled the windows down and our jaws dropped, literally. There was a palace. No, it was *the* palace. It was incredibly fantastic. It rose perhaps seventy feet from the ground. It stretched as far as the eye could see. The Royal Palace had high stone walls and there were three towers in it, two of which were about eighty feet high with the middle one about a hundred feet tall. There were flags at the top of each building inside the Palace that carried the Royal City's symbol.

I loved beautiful buildings, but suddenly I felt darkness. It was separate from the darkness I'd memorised, less powerful, more mischievous.

"What's wrong?" Alpheus asked me. I guessed that the presence was too weak for them to feel it yet, but Alpheus must have suspected something. I would have expected nothing less of Alpheus.

"There is a dark mage here," I replied tensely.

Chapter 12

TROUBLE IN PARADISE

W e drove on in silence, still admiring the buildings in Royal City. We couldn't help it, despite the fact that there was a dark mage in the city. The buildings were so purely masterpieces of art that we just kept up the admiring. The theme of the buildings was colonial, that much was obvious.

There were loads of people on the streets. There were flea markets here and there and it all looked very grand. It was as majestic as Settleburg was modern.

"I want to perform a cleansing Ritual from the top of the highest tower in the Royal Palace," I said longingly with a sigh. I rested my head against the window frame and let the wind blow over my face. "I really, really want to." My entire body seemed to long for it, in fact. It felt as if my power was trying to drag my body to the tower from inside me.

"Perhaps we can go there later today," Alpheus said comfortingly.

"We need to stock up on food," Gwenwyn said instantly. We laughed.

"Is food the only thing you ever think about?" Ezra grumbled.

"You grumble too much; you're like an old man," Gwenwyn complained.

"I *am* an old man," Ezra retorted right back.

"Enough, you guys," Quinteth said, rolling her eyes. She tied her hair up in a high pony tail. Her fiery red hair hung down her back and framed her face showing off her high cheekbones.

I tied my hair up as well. It was noon, and Royal City had a high temperature. My bangs came down to my eyes, too short to be tied up. Gwenwyn had no trouble with her hair, because it remained light. I realised that our hair was a complete contrast. Mine was blacker than night, and hers was almost as white as snow with the barest hints of yellow.

Alpheus found an inn that looked the smallest, but it was still bigger than Settleburg's inn. It was about four storeys high and very wide. He parked inside and we went in, each bringing a small bag with clothes and toiletries to last us for two days. I brought some Ritual ingredients as well, sincerely hoping to be able to perform a Ritual from the highest tower.

It had something to do with my Bound power. The higher I go, the better the effects, the greater the pleasure. Man, that sounded like a scientific conclusion.

We got two small rooms again, and each room had two single beds. I agreed to share one bed with Gwenwyn because I was smaller than Quinteth, so there would be comfortable space. We didn't bother unpacking and straightaway went to the inn's mini restaurant. The main courses were all meaty food and we were grateful for it after eating canned food for two weeks.

I looked around the restaurant and the first thing I noticed about the people was that they were very laid back.

They wore grand clothes but chatted and gestured in a very casual manner. Once we were done with our five course feast, we went out of the Visitor's Inn and started in the direction of the Royal Palace.

The city was getting dark but there were lights. Loads and loads of lights decorated the majestic city, making it glimmer and shine. We found our way to the Royal Palace easily, because it was so huge. I was certain that anyone could see it from anywhere in the city.

However, when we reached the Royal Palace, we were faced with a problem. The guards wouldn't let us in.

"No visitors after six," said one of the guards. There were three more guards standing there, backing him up.

"I got this," Quinteth assured us. She stepped forwards and twirled her hair around her finger and flipped it back. She smiled at them alluringly. "I'm sorry we came so late, officers. It's my entire fault; I took too long changing. You see, I wanted to look nice when my pictures are taken here." She looked sad. "I guess it was all for nothing. Thank you officers for doing your work." She smiled at them, and was turning halfway when the guard that stopped us spoke up. Their eyes were glued to her sexy figure.

"Uh, miss? Perhaps we could let you all in, since it is only half past six. But the best we can give you is half an hour," he added, his voice turning adamant towards the end.

"Really?" Quinteth fluttered her long dark lashes. "I'm so grateful to you gentleman."

They were all smiles when they stepped aside to let us in. Once we were out of earshot, Ezra started sniggering.

"*Officers?*" he snickered. We were all giggling uncontrollably. "Well, that was easy."

"How did you do it?" Gwenwyn asked her. Quinteth shrugged nonchalantly.

"It's just something I had learned about the men of the past two centuries. Their desires are greater than their duties," she explained. We all fell back into the giggling fits. Alpheus just smiled indulgently.

"Who's there?" a strong male voice called out. We froze, our eyes searching for the owner of the voice. It was human as far as I could tell. Then we made out a silhouette.

"We are visitors," Quinteth tried. The figure gave a humourless laugh, and stepped into the light. We were facing the prince of Royal City's Royal Palace.

"Visitors aren't allowed in after six," he said grandly. I tried checking him out, and he looked like everything a prince should look like. He had perfectly styled blond hair, a golden tanned skin and he was dressed impeccably neat. "Perhaps it is time to hire some new guards."

"It's my fault; I coerced them into letting me in," Quinteth said quickly. We felt uneasy. We did want to come in, but we didn't want to get anyone in trouble.

"Is that so? Did you threaten them with their lives?" he looked unimpressed. "Well, since you are already inside, it would be ungracious of me to not be your guide."

I frowned. I wouldn't be able to cast shit with a prince with us.

"No, it's alright," I said, stepping forward. His eyes widened as he looked at me. "We will just come back tomorrow."

"Wait," he gasped out when I turned to go. I looked at him, a questioning look on my face. "Are you . . . could you possibly be Crescentia Al Nyhaivhar?" he asked, and the awe in his voice was evident. We were all shocked into silence.

"How do you know?" I lowered my voice.

"So it is you!" he walked forward quickly and grasped my hands, making Alpheus step forward. "I need your help," He continued, ignoring Alpheus.

"What?"

Ten minutes later, we were in the grand ballroom of the Royal Palace, enjoying the impressionist art and the general structure of the room. We were sitting on a large couch, about the size of a king-sized bed. In our hands were cups of warm tea. I'd secretly added a bit of lavender into my cup and was enjoying it immensely.

The prince had left us there, telling us to wait. He wanted to show us something. We sipped our tea and waited in silence.

"Do you feel that?" Ezra asked. Nobody responded. It was obvious to everyone that a dark mage had been here. Not in this ballroom, particularly, but in the Palace grounds. The presence was very vague, but it was there. The dark mage wasn't here at this moment, though.

When the prince entered, he didn't enter alone.

We stood quickly to face the King and Queen of Royal City. We all curtsied, the guys bowed.

"Rise," the King boomed. He looked like a dark haired version of his son. We straightened up out of our curtsies and walked forward.

The King and Queen couldn't take their eyes off of my face. The prince obviously got his hair colour and skin tone from his mother.

"It is you, Crescentia," the Queen breathed. I was confused. How do they know me?

"I'm sorry, but I do not know you," I said sincerely. They looked unsurprised by my statement.

"Of course you wouldn't know us. You would perhaps know our great ancestor William Fitzgerald?" the King asked me respectfully. I could sense approval from my friends for the way they treated me.

The name William Fitzgerald rang a bell. "I think he was someone I had helped before."

"You saved his life," the prince corrected.

"That's right," I remembered slowly. "He was threatened by a dark mage who was after the crown jewels."

"Yes, that's it," the King said. "That is what he wrote in his journal. You really are Crescentia, and so we owe you our lives for saving our crown. However, as much as we want to offer you the world, we need to ask a favour."

"The dark mage is back?" I guessed.

They looked surprised, and then naturally suspicious. "How do you know that, Miss Crescentia?" the King asked.

"I can feel him. It isn't the same one though," I said casually. "It must be a relative after the same thing."

They looked awed. "How do you know it isn't the same one?" the prince questioned.

I wasn't going to tell them how I could tell the difference between presences, so I told them the easier one instead. "The one I defeated is still Bound, and always will be."

"I see," the prince said, looking nothing of such. The King and Queen also looked mystified but were willing to accept my words.

"Well, it seems that the wards you placed came away sixteen years ago, for no reason that we could think of, and now we're being threatened again. The thief comes in every night for the past sixteen years and steals something from the palace as long as we wouldn't give it the crown jewels," the King said in frustration.

"It is in the highest tower," I said easily.

"What?" the Queen gasped.

"I am guessing, but none of you have searched the rooms in the highest tower for the past sixteen years, is that right?"

I said. They nodded as one, intrigued. "This is because the dark mage has stored the things there and placed a repellent spell so that nobody would feel like going there."

"No wonder I despised the idea of going there for the past sixteen years." The Queen breathed. "What about the wards?" she asked.

I pressed my lips tightly. "That is something I cannot tell. But do not worry, the dark mage will only come at night, and he will not come tonight, not after sensing me here," I assured them.

They looked like they were assured. Then again, I was their ancestor's saviour.

"It is late, we should get some rest," Gwenwyn said. I looked at the clock and it said eight p.m. Wow, it has been two hours since we left the Visitor's Inn. Gwenwyn must be starving.

"You may stay here, if you want," the King of Royal Palace offered.

"It's alright. We will return now," I said. "We will be back by noon tomorrow."

The prince ushered us out. The maids and manservants that brought our tea to us were nowhere in sight.

"Keep my existence a secret," I told the prince, knowing full well what those words would mean to him. "All my friends and I."

He nodded, looking at me in awe. It was the words I had said to William Fitzgerald when we parted. There was a difference, though. Back then, I was only Bound to Snowy. We left the palace and assured the guards that they weren't in trouble, because they had spotted the prince.

Gwenwyn went to the mini restaurant at the inn straightaway and Quinteth followed her, not wanting her to be alone with a dark mage in the same city as us. I didn't doubt that the dark mage could sense us as well. I went up to my room and Ezra went into the boy's room. Alpheus followed me in.

"What had happened with William Fitzgerald?" he asked in curiosity. I sat on the bed and patted the sheet beside me. He came and sat.

"Well, I don't remember how long this was. It was after I met Gwenwyn but before I met you," I told him. I had met Gwenwyn before the rest of them and then Alpheus, followed by Quinteth then Ezra. "The dark mage wanted the crown jewels because they were special. They were made from reinforced tanzanite and were enchanted to sparkle with a glow."

Ezra's head popped in and I nodded, allowing him to enter. He was obviously interested to listen to the story.

"However, the spell was Uncasted, so it made the jewels powerful. If it fell into the hands of a dark mage, their powers would increase tenfold. But the dark mages couldn't compel William to give it to them because the spell repelled them. He had to give it to them willingly, but they were able to threaten everyone he held dear."

"At that time, this place was just a large village with a stone castle. Witches and sorcerers were out in the open, no need to hide. That was back when we lived at peace with the humans, and they saw us as equals. This was really long ago," I said thoughtfully, "When the dark mages hadn't terrorised the humans, causing them to distrust us."

"He appealed to me for help, and as I was staying there as a guest, I couldn't refuse the King of the castle. So I waited for the dark mage to appear. I held onto the crown as bait and when he came, it was a simple matter to cast a Binding spell. It's not the same spell as the one I used on all of you," I said, noticing their surprise. "This one was to strip him of his powers and keep him underground. It was easy in those times because everything was simple and unpolluted by humans. Magic was everywhere."

I smiled ruefully. "I hadn't even needed to draw a pentagram."

"So, why did your wards stop working?" Ezra asked.

"Don't you know?" I asked. "Because I was reborn. The Binding spell will last forever, but not the wards. The wards were coded specifically to Crescentia's magic patterns. Even though I am a reincarnation, I am not exactly the original Crescentia."

They nodded, but I wondered if they really understood.

"Well!" I said. "It's time to go to bed. See you guys tomorrow." I tapped them on the back and they left. I had to get Alpheus away from me especially when we were on the same bed. I turned off the light and lay down on my bed. I only fell asleep once Quinteth and Gwenwyn were safely in the room with me.

The next day, we all woke up at around half past ten. It was probably unhealthy of us, but the feel of sleeping in a bed and not the jeep seats were luxurious. We were ready to leave the inn after breakfast by eleven thirty and set off. It was different to view the Royal City in broad daylight. It was really nothing short of a structural miracle.

We reached the palace at noon on the dot. The guards were different now, and we were let in easily since it was visiting hours. We walked about five paces when we saw the prince approach us from afar. He waved and smiled when he saw me.

He stopped in front of us. "Would you like the King and Queen to accompany you?" he asked. "They are in a meeting with the prime minister right now, but at your words, they would end it and follow you." He seemed to be ignoring my friends.

I took a step back. "There is no need for that. I need to apologize; I'd forgotten to introduce my friends. This is Alpheus, Gwenwyn, Quinteth and Ezra."

He nodded at them in turn, out of respect for me. I got the feeling that he couldn't really care less about them, and I didn't like it. I took a step towards him and smiled. This smile was a dangerous one. Remora had called it my vampire smile, because it looked like fangs would sprout from my gums when I smiled this way. He took two quick steps back unconsciously.

"Perhaps you should not come with us," I told him, my tone leaving no doubt that there wasn't a choice anyway. "It is not a sight for mortal eyes."

"Yes, of course," he said. I had to give him credit; he was quick to recover and regain composure. "Do you need me to at least escort you there?"

I shook my head. "I need your permission for one thing though." When I told him, he thought about it.

"Go for it," he finally decided. "Our safety is more important anyway."

I nodded and we took off, running. We were running because we felt the dark mage's presence at the top of the tower. Dark mages generally didn't have names, until they became powerful enough to earn one, so we always had to refer to the dark mages as 'dark mages'.

"*Winds of power, give us flight!*" I commanded as soon as we were inside the tower and out of public eyes, and our feet no longer touched the ground. Power boosted from the soles of our feet and propelled us forward. There was magic in this air. I felt the dark mage's alarm once he sensed us in the tower.

I felt a pentagram being drawn quickly and a wall of tight air was thrown at us. I dispelled it with a wave of my hand, coated with power. The wind knocked against the wall and scattered, vanishing. The next pentagram was quickly drawn, and a fireball was thrown down towards us.

I waved it away again with my hand coated with power. The power was strong, so I had to wave at it twice before it was thrown into the wall. I heard a gasp and knew that Gwenwyn was hit with the resonating sparks. I threw some power over my shoulder, willing it to hit her and heal her. I could feel it working. The tower was really high up, we probably just only passed the halfway mark.

Then a tsunami was thrown at us. I raised both hands, palms out and held it at bay. I was actually trying to turn the tide before realising that the dark mage had made it irreversible. So I closed my palms tight, crushing the tsunami which evaporated instantly. If I wasn't a Great Witch, I would have been drained completely of my powers by now. However, I was just getting warmed up.

I added speed to our flight and felt the fourth pentagram being drawn. A large boulder came rolling down the steps at high speed. I stared at it in surprise. This dark mage was more powerful than I'd thought. He must have tried to Shield some of his power. As soon as I knew this was right, the Shield was invisible to me and I felt his presence in full force.

It was a powerful dark mage, but it wasn't powerful enough to be named, I was sure. However, a dark mage of this level may seriously injure one of my friends. I made a split decision and closed my eyes, muttering a quick spell. As I muttered, the boulder grew bigger and bigger until it completely blocked off the space and I made myself insubstantial at the same time I stopped my friends' flight.

I sailed right through the boulder and heard my friends protest loudly.

"I'm sorry, my friends," I apologised. I felt them draw a pentagram and joined hands to get rid of the boulder, but I didn't have time to worry about them anymore. I had burst into the room at the top of the tower, and came face to face with the dark mage who was frantically drawing a pentagram. *"Be still!"* I commanded, drawing on my power and unleashing it on him.

No matter how many times I saw a dark mage, I could never get over how ugly they were. White mages favoured nature and were given human forms to contribute to goodness and peace. Dark mages, however, went against everything that was important to the power and became ugly creatures.

I looked at this one now. There were criss-cross scars across his rotten face and his teeth were black and chipped. His lips were a dark blue and his body was shrouded in the general black attire they sported. It kept them comfortable. His bare hands were disfigured where they stilled over the half-drawn pentagram.

"Great White Mage," he hissed, foul black smoke coming out of his mouth. "The Great One is coming for you."

"Who is this Great One?" I demanded, but I already knew. I didn't want to believe it, but his words confirmed my suspicions.

He laughed, and the sound was like broken glass. "It is the Great Bethamzar! He has great powers, and he will destroy you!"

I scrunched my nose against the disgusting smell from the black smoke that came out of his mouth, shoving aside the feelings that his words invoked in me. "How will he do that?" I demanded with authority.

"I'll not tell you!" he hissed loudly. "I'll not tell you!"

I smiled again then. He looked scared of me for the first time since we laid eyes on each other. I was wearing my vampire smile.

I quickly drew a pentagram in the air with my fingers, and it pushed itself against the dark mage, tightening around his throat.

"Are you going to kill me, Great White Witch?" he rasped loudly in his horrible voice.

"I will do much worse than that!" I yelled, and my voice was coated with power. Suddenly, there were winds in the room, and it whipped my hair about. *"I will do much worse than that!"* I repeated loudly, and I knew he truly feared me now. My eyes had another colour that I had forgotten to mention, but it only happened when I was casting spells. My irises turned brilliant blood-red and glowed.

"Pardon Great Witch!" he cried. "Pardon!"

"How will he destroy me?" I roared.

"By your own power!" he cried helplessly. "He will use your power, but that's all I know! I swear! Pardon Great Witch!"

"O dark mage, enemy of light, enemy of good, enemy of will," I chanted, my hands working fast, drawing pentagram after pentagram. The Binding spells required seven specific pentagrams in sequence, one after another. *"O dark mage, accursed the day you turned, striped of power, stored in sour,"* I drew the last pentagram as the winds stopped completely. It was the calm before the storm.

"I release thee from thy power!" I declared, screaming the words at the top of my lungs. The pentagrams were all activated, and he was trapped inside them. A great gale shook the entire tower, and every window shattered. The dark mage became insubstantial and was transported deep into the earth where he would never regain his power, together with many dark mages I have sent there.

This was one of my special powers. I was Bound to release the dark mages of their power so that the balance of the world would be restored. Nature itself would hold the dark mages in the earth, rendering them unconscious and powerless forever as punishment. There was always a choice to become a dark mage. Once a mage turned, there was no going back.

I looked around the room, and noticed that there was quite a lot of treasure here. I was right; the dark mage had stored it all here. I heard the sound of my friends' footsteps echoing. They burst into the room in panic, only to find me holding up a painting, admiring it.

"Oh, you're here," I said casually, showing them the painting. Their faces were sour and they didn't spare a single glance at it. "You wouldn't have been able to do anything," I told them. When they looked like they were about to argue, I levelled a look at them. It was my no-nonsense face and their protests died in their throat. "Look," I coaxed softly.

They glared at me for a second longer before looking, and then they did a double take. Even Alpheus looked surprised. Gwenwyn stepped forward to admire it.

"It is you," she said. I nodded. Apparently William had gotten an artist to draw me. It was goatskin, so this was from my time. I mean, it was from Crescentia's time.

Alpheus walked forward and hugged me tightly, and his frantically thudding heart slowed down. "Don't ever do that again," he bit out. And I couldn't find it in myself to disappoint him.

"Okay," I promised.

We went back down to a worried prince and King and Queen.

"All the windows are shattered." The prince observed worriedly, looking at me in concern. "Windows can be fixed easily, but are you hurt?" they had obviously closed the palace off, because there were no tourists inside the palace walls.

"I am alright," I said easily. I was at perhaps three quarters tank of power, not including the power I had on reserve, which meant I still had about eighty per cent of my power intact. "Take me to the crown."

The prince nodded. The King looked worried. "Why do you want the crown?"

"I will show you," was all I said.

Once we were inside and I was facing the crown, the brilliant purple tanzanite stones shone at me. I felt the promise of power from the stones. I laid my hands on the crown.

"*Spell of right, reach of dark, go to light, hide the dark,*" I said, and closed my eyes. I felt the spell shudder under the weight of my words of power. I coaxed the spell out from the stones and a purple mist floated above the crown. I closed my fist over it and destroyed it with power. It vanished without a trace.

Chapter 13

BETHAMZAR'S CURSE, MY PAST

O nce our business was done in Royal City, I told the King that I would hold on to their offer of giving me the world. They had laughed, but I was only half-joking. One always needed a backup plan. That night itself I had forced us to pack up and travel again, the urge to get to the bottom of this stronger than ever.

Because I knew who Bethamzar was, and he was not an easy foe. White mages could never become Great Witches if they weren't born to the power. However, dark mages were a different story. The more ruthless they were, the more powerful they became. The worst part was that white witches had a choice to turn dark, and once they were turned, the process was final, and sometimes fatal.

Bethamzar was a different story. He was born as a Great White Sorcerer but certain events led to his change into a Great Dark Mage. The symbol that he bore was a dragon. Mine was a phoenix, and that was why I was able to be reincarnated.

As Alpheus drove, I was quiet in the shotgun seat. They all knew that the dark mage had told me something serious.

After three hours of indecisive brooding, I finally made the decision to confide in them.

"The dark mage told me that the foe we seek is called Bethamzar," I said quietly. There was a sharp intake of breath.

"It's a named dark mage?" Ezra hissed. I could see both Quinteth and Gwenwyn pale until they were as white as bone.

"There is more," I whispered, and my voice was shaky. This was the epitome of my nightmares. It was worse than being burned at the stake. I was finally going to reveal my darkest secret.

Alpheus's hand found my knee and he squeezed it lightly, reassuringly. But even he didn't know the horror that I was about to reveal.

"He was born a Great White Sorcerer," I said slowly, building up to it. They had similar looks of terror now. Mages that were born to the power was no joke. "And . . ." I swallowed. "And he is my brother."

They all stilled, even Alpheus's hand on my knee went cold.

"We're doomed." Ezra said weakly. "A son of the Grand White Mage who has turned is entirely too powerful. We will go to our deaths."

There was silence after that. Alpheus left his hand on my knee to comfort me until I couldn't take it and put it back on the wheel. I faced the window and brooded solemnly, thinking about my past, aeons ago.

* * *

"Shhh," Bethamzar shushed me, giggling slightly. I had my own smile pressed onto my face, trying to stop my giggles. We were hiding low in a thick bush, slightly high

127

up so that we could look at the people below us but they couldn't see us. "Look yonder, Crescentia!" he whispered, pointing.

We saw our mother, calmly walking down the street, nodding to the village folk left and right. They all knew her, and they all loved her. I took a moment to truly look at her and knew that she was beautiful. She had long, glossy locks of waving black hair; her skin was porcelain white, like the precious china in our house. Her eyes were big and exotically shaped, framed with thick dark lashes. Her mouth was full and naturally red and she had pale pink cheeks.

"Bethamzar, Crescentia," she called and we quickly hid deeper into the bush. It was her birthday today, and we hid her present with us, wanting to surprise her, but it was quite impossible to surprise a Grand Mage. I saw her eyes instantly jump to our bush as soon as it was in sight, but she must have guessed what we were up to. A small smile crept up her lips and she looked away, pretending not to know.

As a seven year old child, I didn't know she was pretending, and we smiled triumphantly at each other. Once she was out of earshot, we sat back comfortably.

"What are we to tell her?" I asked the eight year old Bethamzar. "We cannot say that we went to Willow's Creek to collect the berries."

"Why ever not?" he asked, amazed. I shook my head at him. Sometimes he was too playful to think things through.

"We cannot reach the berries," I told him. "She will know we used the power, and she will be angry."

He frowned, nodding. "Thou art right. Our hands do not have the stain of the berries either."

"I know!" I exclaimed excitedly. "We can say that we asked someone else to pick them for us."

"Okay," he agreed easily. "We can say Christopheri did it."

Christopheri was our secret friend whom no one knew about. We always felt awkward around him, but he played with us and taught us so many fun games that we ignored the feeling. He forbade us to tell anyone about him, even our mother, but he said we could use his name as a scapegoat.

I agreed and asked him if it was alright for us to get down now. He popped his head out to scan the area and gave the all clear. We climbed down and went to our house quickly. We saw that our mother had not yet returned and we quickly decorated our basket of blackberries with pretty flowers.

And then we waited for our mother to return home. She eventually came home with a basket of groceries. We stood at the door and beamed at her hugely, hiding the basket behind our backs.

"Yes, what is the matter?" she asked us sweetly, amused. She set her basket down and faced us.

We looked at each other and Bethamzar mouthed 'one, two, and three'.

"Surprise!" We cried, showing her our basketful of berries. She clapped delightedly, and exaggerated joy to indulge us. "Happy Birthday, Mother."

"Oh, thou art lovelies! Thank thee very much." She admired our handiwork of flowers.

"We got the berries so that thou may make a birthday cake for thyself." Bethamzar said sincerely, dimples on either side of his angelic face when he smiled.

Our mother laughed and told us that she would bake it right away. Bethamzar helped her stoke the fire and I helped her knead the dough.

That night, as we lay in bed, we heard a voice calling out to us in our minds. It was Christopheri. We looked at each other and went out quietly, trying not to alert our mother. We held hands as we sprinted out the door and onto the road in our bare feet. Once we reached the Hollow, the cluster of trees with a large hollow one in the middle, we stopped. Christopheri lived in the Hollow.

"Greetings, children," his raspy voice hissed. As children, we didn't think much of it. It sounded like the voice of an old human. He wore a mask over his face.

"Greetings, Christopheri," we replied. We didn't go too near him because it made us feel a bit dizzy.

"What hath thou been up to?" he asked in his shattered voice.

"We celebrated our mother's birthday," I told him proudly. "We got the berries from Willow's Creek all by ourselves."

"Did thee now?" he rasped. "How did thou do it? I do not think thou hath grown since yesterday."

"We used our power," Bethamzar said with pride. We were both happy to tell someone of our achievements.

"How did thou use it?" he asked. He sat down and we sat on the ground.

"I do not know," Bethamzar said. I smiled and raised my hand.

"I do know," I said. "We pull on our inner power and shoot it out of our hands and it catches the berries and the berries float into the basket."

Christopheri clapped. "Very good!" his eyes pierced into mine and I shrunk back a bit. "Thou hath developed quite well."

Bethamzar patted me on the back and I smiled. Then Christopheri taught us a new childish game and we played until the dawn. Once the sun showed its first rays, Christopheri sent us off.

"It is time to go home," He said. "Do not forget to perform a cleansing Ritual."

"We will!" Bethamzar said and we left, going to Willow's Creek. We held one hand and the other we put into the creek's water.

"Cleanse us; water, from all filth, inside, outside, every side," we chanted. It was a child's spell, designed so that it was easy for us to remember. We felt ourselves purified and our dizziness from Christopheri's presence disappeared.

We went home quickly and got into our beds just as our mother woke up. She came into our room and frowned, perhaps noticing that something was wrong, but then she let it go and went to make breakfast. We looked at each other and shared a cheeky conspiratorial smile.

Over the course of the next few years, we learnt many things from our mother and I bloomed into the power much faster than Bethamzar. Whenever a villager needed help, I was the first one they turned to. Even Christopheri favoured me over my brother, and he grew jealous and bitter, but I didn't know until it was too late.

One night, my mother was supposed to name the one she wanted to succeed the important power of Binding, and she unsurprisingly named me. My brother congratulated me heartily and told me he would be off to tell Christopheri while my mother taught me the pentagrams and words. But I didn't know that he went to Christopheri to vent his frustration at me.

We had already begin to suspect what Christopheri was; a dark mage. But we couldn't be sure because we were inexperienced. He didn't have the dark presence as the ones our mother Bound. Upon hearing the news that Bethamzar brought, Christopheri seized his chance.

The next day, Bethamzar went missing and our mother performed the tracking Ritual. I watched anxiously, waiting for news of my beloved brother. When she was done, she stumbled to the ground and stayed there, stunned.

"How did this happen?" she whispered in horror.

"What happened, Mother?" I asked, filled with fear. I feared what I thought had been the worst, that Bethamzar was dead. There had been rumours of the village being terrorised by a dark mage, so I feared that Bethamzar had been caught.

She turned her piercing orange-green eyes on me. "Hath thou been in the presence of a dark mage?"

"No!" I protested, but my mind flew to Christopheri.

"Who doth that be?" my mother advanced towards me and held my shoulders, shaking me. She had seen my thoughts. "Who doth that be?" she demanded.

"It is Christopheri!" I cried out quickly, scared.

"Where did thou meet him?" she adamantly demanded, her expression filled with horror.

"He lives at the Hollow," I blurted, knowing that this had something to do with Bethamzar, so I didn't feel guilty about breaking my promise. If Christopheri had done something to my brother . . .

"He is a Great Dark Mage!" my mother flew into a rage and ran into the kitchen, gathering spell ingredients. "He Shielded his presence from thy Sight, and thou grew used to it. I do not blame thee. But we must hurry, or something terrible will happen to thy brother." She stuffed the ingredients into a sheepskin sack and threw it to me. I caught it.

"Hurry to where?" I asked, mystified. "What will happen to Bethamzar?"

"The Hollow!" my mother replied. She rushed out the door and I rushed after her. We ran with all our might, and my mother even used magic to increase our speed. That was when I knew things were bad, because my mother never used magic for personal gain.

We reached the Hollow, and a fearsome sight awaited us.

Bethamzar was levitating inside the hollow tree, his eyes closed and his skin glowed with red light. Christopheri's mask was off, and he was the ugliest thing I had ever seen. He had patches of multi-coloured hair and rotten skin, and whenever he opened his mouth, black smoke came out.

And then I noticed something that made my heart stop. Bethamzar was bleeding. He was bleeding from his eyes, from his ears and from his mouth. I screamed.

My mother quickly drew pentagrams in the air and muttered the magic words with a speed that was astounding. Right before Christopheri was caught in the net of Binding pentagrams, he threw a cursed blade at Bethamzar that stabbed him directly in the heart.

Blood exploded from his chest and sprayed out into the air and red filled my vision. Blood was everywhere, and it splattered against my face and arms and kidskin clothes.

"Thou art too late!" Christopheri laughed and the sound hurt my ears, like shattering glass. "Thou art too late, my dear wife!"

"Not yet, not yet!" my mother shouted. I was stunned to learn that Christopheri was our father. She Bound Christopheri and I watched as his skin turned back to normal, his ugliness cured as she striped his power from him. "Crescentia, go purify thy brother, make haste!"

I was terrified, but I forced my frozen legs to move towards Bethamzar. His body was jerking violently, blood still splurging from the blade. I felt defiled as soon as I saw that blade. This was a deeply cursed blade; one that had ripped the lives of many innocents. The blade seemed to be going into his body, and at the same time drawing his blood out. It was a Dragon Blade.

I quickly drew the purifying pentagram in the air and grabbed the lavender from the ingredients. There was no fire here for me to call on, and my powers were not yet precise.

If I called on fire, I may accidentally burn the entire village. So I compensated, doing the next best thing. I bit my thumb and drew blood.

I quickly smeared it on the lavender and waved it over my pentagram. There was a lot of magic in the air, but it was all defiled and filled with darkness. *"White light call forth, white power bring forth, white —"* before I could finish the chant, I was blown backwards. It seemed a great burst of power had pulsed outwards from Bethamzar's body.

My mother stood her ground and she drew pentagrams and chanted at high speed. All I saw was red, and there was a ringing in my ears. Bethamzar's blood became solid, and it looked like red ribbons sprouting out of his chest and arched high before touching the ground. It kept him in a red cage.

Just a few more words, I heard my mother's voice in my head. *Come, daughter, I need thy help.*

I struggled to get up but it felt like there was an elephant sitting on me. I screamed, frustrated, putting my palms flat below me and trying to push myself up. The pressure that was pushing me down grew and I hit the ground flat again, coughing up blood. I felt blood run down my nose as well.

I was bewildered. What was happening?! My mother kept on drawing and chanting, going closer to him step by step. The pressure on my body increased and I couldn't breathe. I somehow understood that it would be over if I could help my mother.

I fought against the pressure, pushing my palm out to face my mother. I concentrated and threw my power towards her. Her speed was heightened until she managed to get right up to my brother. She finished the last spell and put her hand on his chest, desperately trying to take out the cursed blade. Her hands kept slipping over the blood.

I felt my backbone crack and I screamed in pain. There was a tremendous searing in between my shoulder blades.

My power instantly went to heal me. My lungs were magically filled with air and I could breathe again. I looked up just in time to see my mother's horrified face when the blade slipped out of her hand and sink completely into Bethamzar. Then everything stopped.

There was no longer any pressure on my back and I got up weakly, staggering to my mother who stood frozen, staring at the face of my brother. Tears ran down her face. Bethamzar was no longer levitating; his body lay on the ground.

"I was too late," she whispered and looked at me with wide eyes. "So thou art the phoenix and he is the dragon." She looked terrified at the revelation. And then Bethamzar opened his blood-red eyes. Those were our power eyes.

He smiled at us both. "Hello, mother. Hello, sister." And I understood what had happened when I watched as his skin started to rot and ugly patterns filled his face. The black smoke that came out of his mouth was warning enough.

And then he did the unthinkable. He punched his hand through my mother's chest and pulled out her heart. She gave one gasp and fell to the ground. I backed away quickly from the horror. He threw her heart away in disgust. He had his first kill, so he was officially blooded. There was no turning back now.

"It is thy turn, sister," he rasped. I caught sight of my unfinished pentagram, floating in the air.

"I think not," I said, and finished my pentagram. A pure light burst forth from the pentagram and I ran, Shielding myself as best as I could. He howled in pain as the purifying light filled his body. I pushed all my power into the purifying pentagram, but just before I closed the deal, his eyes found mine, and we locked eyes. In that moment, I saw us as children, and I couldn't end him.

I changed it at the last millisecond, into a Binding spell instead. It was a decision I would regret for the rest of my life. The purifying spell mixed with the Binding spell and weakened him greatly, but they also cancelled each other out. He collapsed onto the ground, steaming from every pore. I ran forward, my only thought was to rip the blade out of him at any cost, but before I could do that, the blade shattered in his body, spreading throughout his veins. It was as though the blade knew what I was about to do; and it wouldn't let me.

I cursed. Now I couldn't get it out as one piece. I threw a white sage at him but it was fried before it touched him. He was Shielded, and there was nothing more I could do. I'd given everything I had into stopping him, but it would only keep him down for a few ten thousand years, at best.

I ran back to my house and got a shovel. I went back to the Hollow and dug for hours and hours until the hole was double my height, and I got out and used the shovel to shove him inside. I covered it back and hoped that nature would do its job.

I found my mother's body and her heart, and I tried to place it back in her body, and then buried her next to my brother. I hoped that her pure being would also help keep him contained.

And then I washed every part of myself in Willow's Creek, scrubbing and scrubbing and scrubbing, but I couldn't do the same for my mind. The blood of my family filled my thoughts and haunted me for years to come. I left the village secretly and went around aimlessly, helping those in need, Binding dark mages and trying to get stronger in fear that my brother would one day be awakened.

Chapter 14

REVELATION IN SOUTH HUNTERS WOODS

There was only one way to enter Rigs City, and that was to go through South Hunters Woods. I stored my deep emotions of fear about Bethamzar deep inside me so that my dark mood wouldn't affect my friends. They were depressed enough as it is, yet I never detected any thoughts of abandoning this journey. I was deeply touched by their loyalty to me.

The road forked into two, one was to go straight onwards to Littlestown, and the other to the left, where the South Hunters Woods awaited. The road to the South Hunters Woods was narrow and bumpy, like it hadn't been used for a very long time.

Rigs City was the smallest of all the three main cities in the Regions, but they were very well self-sustained. I doubted many people left their city. I'd learnt in Settleburg High School that the people of Rigs City were proud and patriotic, so they rarely ever mixed with any other part of the Regions.

The road slowly turned into a jungle trek and I could feel all of our relief that we used a jeep instead of a car. I gritted my teeth against the irritating jerking as the jeep bounced over roots and whatnot. Trees blocked off the early afternoon sunlight and it was abruptly very dark.

There were creepy insect sounds all around us and there were trees and vines as far as the eye could see. I pressed my fingers to my forehead, uncomfortable with the thick gloom that filled the jungle air.

There were so many dark mage presences here, but there was also another presence intertwined with it all. It was, beyond a doubt, the Hunters.

I knew because I'd met a few over the years. But I'd only met the ones in the North Hunters Woods. I wasn't sure if they held the same ideals, or were on opposite ends.

The village I was born in was inside Rigs City, but it was aeons ago. I had no idea how it would look like now. Also, I'd truly never been in South Hunters Woods throughout my entirely too long life, for the simple reason that there had never been a reason to. When I'd left Rigs City back then, there were other routes out of the place.

"So what's the deal with this Beth—" Ezra finally burst out.

"Shhh!" I cut Ezra off. I felt question marks in all their heads and I sighed. "It is best not to say anything dark in these woods. We might accidentally summon them."

That shut them up real quick.

"He turned," I relented, choosing my words carefully and trying not to think about him. "I really can't describe it without saying dark things, so I think it will have to wait until we reach Rigs City. There is a place that is under a permanent light spell, so we can speak of it there."

"How do you know?" Gwenwyn asked, surprised. "Did you find it in the tracking spell?"

I shook my head. "I know because my mother was the one who casted the spell."

They were silent for a while, absorbing this new information. Now they knew that my hometown was in Rigs City, and I felt their excitement despite the current situation. "It didn't used to be called Rigs City, you know," I told them, smiling a little. "It was little better than a caveman-style village."

I was about to continue when I felt many presences spying on us from the shadows of the trees. The Hunters were here. "But that story can wait."

They understood that I didn't want to say anything because the Hunters would hear. I doubted the three on the backseat knew what Hunters were though. They had never met a Hunter before, except Alpheus. I peeked at him and he had a stoic face on.

Good or bad? I asked him.

Neither, he replied. *They are just observing.*

In case we're up to anything funny?

Alpheus frowned, staring out the windshield. His eyes darted pretty much everywhere. *They are gathering.*

For what? I was getting worried. Negative emotions were rarely ever displayed on Alpheus's face, and now that he was frowning, I wondered if it was time to panic.

Alpheus didn't respond to my thoughts. His frown deepened and the jeep picked up speed as he leaned on the gas. I could feel worry coming from the backseat, but I wasn't sure if it would be a lie to tell them there was nothing to worry about.

After all, Alpheus was frowning.

I could feel the Hunters' presences thicken like fog. They were really gathering, but whatever for?

Then the jeep screeched to a stop and I was thrown against the harness and back into the seat. Quinteth, who was sitting behind me, slammed into the back of my seat. All our eyes went to the person standing in front of the jeep.

I looked at Alpheus and he had his poker face on.

What's going on? I asked him, worried.

They want to talk, he replied.

About what?

Let's find out, he grimaced.

On that positive note, the dark figure beckoned us to exit to jeep. I bit my lip, trying to find options, but it was hard because we were completely surrounded. We were out of options, and the only one available was to talk. So, I took a deep breath and nodded, and we climbed out of the jeep.

We walked to the front of the jeep, where the figure was joined by many more. Upon closer inspection, they looked like humans wearing black hooded cloaks. The guy at the front came forward and we saw his face in the dim light. He even put his hood down to smile at us.

He looked young, but probably wasn't. He had dark hair and a pleasant smile, but what stood out the most were his eyes. He had silvery grey eyes, just like Alpheus.

I could feel my friends' wonder as they looked from Alpheus to the guy and back again, comparing their eyes. There was nothing to compare, since the colour was exactly the same. As more of the Hunters became visible, it was obvious that their eyes were a trademark.

Every single one of them had the same eye colour.

"Welcome to South Hunters Woods. My name is Kensington," the guy said. He blinked, turning his silvery eyes on Alpheus, and his smile tightened. "I see we have a northerner. Whatever brings you lovely folks here?"

Alpheus stepped forward, standing in front of me. His silver eyes flashed. "We mean no harm; we are just passing through to go to Rigs City."

Kensington's face darkened. "What business do you have there?" the tone he used was harsh, and the shadows of the other Hunters tightened as they got closer. I bit my lip, worried.

"There is something we must do there," Alpheus said calmly.

Kensington paused and thought for a moment. "Why don't you all introduce yourselves? Give us your full names. And mages please use your original names, not the ones you use as cover."

I stepped around Alpheus to introduce myself, but he pulled me back. Gwenwyn stepped forward instantly.

"My name is Gwenwyn Il Tharhanya. I am a white mage, and I am already Bound."

I suppose I should explain the Binding. For white mages, once you were Bound to a Great White Witch, you were more or less giving your life over. And once you give your life over, you can no longer turn into a dark mage. It was vice versa for the Great Witch. Once the Great Witch has Bound white mage to him or her, the Great Witch could no longer turn dark.

The Hunters looked relieved, and they dropped their hoods. All of them dropped their hoods at once and we stared at them. They all looked completely different from each other, but their silver eyes shone out as one.

Quinteth stepped forward as Gwenwyn stepped back. "I am Quinteth Il Yuilankez. I am a white mage, and I am already Bound."

The Hunters started to frown a little, because of their names. In the ancient times, we were all named after the places we were born in. Of course, names of places changed with time, but it gave the Hunters an idea of how old they were. The places that Gwenwyn and Quinteth were named after were about one thousand and three hundred years ago.

Some of the Hunters were getting pale.

Ezra stepped forward. "My name is Ezra Di Tharhan. I am a white mage, and I am already Bound."

Tharhan was a younger generation of Tharhanya, and that was why it was almost similar. Ezra came from the same place that Gwenwyn did, but he was only born a century later. The place was actually Littlestown now.

Alpheus stood his ground. "My name is Alpheus Di Namphazar. I am a North Hunter, and I am already Bound."

The South Hunters looked at one another in confusion; they didn't know that Hunters could be Bound.

"You are a Bound Hunter?" Kensington asked suspiciously. "Can Hunters be Bound?"

Alpheus nodded. "We can, but only after taking sides and swearing allegiance."

Kensington nodded. "So you are no longer a neutral one."

I stepped forward. "My name is Crescentia Al Nyhaivhar," I said, and watched as more than a few Hunters do double takes. Even Kensington took a step back, staring at me in shock. Nyhaivhar was the first name ever to grace Rigs City. "I am a Great White Mage, and they are all Bound to me."

The resulting silence was deafening. Even the insects didn't make sounds, as if they had understood my words. And then they started to kneel.

I was only mildly surprised. The Hunters in the North Hunters Woods had done the same thing. I was less worried about them now, because they seemed to be quite similar to the North Hunters Woods residents.

"Uh, you can rise," I said quickly, before they could kneel properly. They straightened up again, their faces full of wonder. I guessed that they rarely ever saw an Old One, even though I'm not so old anymore.

"What business does a Great White Mage like you have in Rigs City?" Kensington asked respectfully, bowing slightly. "Do you want to see your hometown?"

I shook my head. "I have to finish what I left behind."

The words hung in the air ominously.

"Do you mean the dark presence in Rigs City?" Kensington asked. More than one Hunter stepped forward eagerly, their eyes shining against the darkness of the forest.

I nodded. "I should have done something a long time ago." I looked down, ashamed of myself. "All the dark mishaps recently is because I could not do what I should have done."

The Hunters seemed to know what I meant. Kensington pursed his lips. "There were many dark mages who passed through. If you go through, this will not be a battle, this will be a war."

I nodded. "I know. I am prepared to do whatever it takes to win the war."

A female Hunter walked forward, and the others gave her a respectful berth. She was ordinary looking, with shoulder length dirty blonde hair and a sharp nose. She walked until she stood right in front of me. I saw something in her eyes that made my breath catch. Alpheus realised who she was at the same time I did, and he stepped away, giving her access to me.

This was no ordinary Hunter. This was the Hunters' clairvoyant.

She reached out her hand and put it against my cheek. I was surprised at the coldness.

"*The tail of the dragon shall impale the phoenix which, in turn, will rise from the ashes.*" She said, her haunting voice echoing loudly in the still forest. Her eyes were glowing brilliantly. "*The rise of the phoenix shall bring great power upon the dragon.*"

She closed her eyes. *"The phoenix shall make a choice, but it will not be raised again."*

She removed her hand from my face, bowed, and backed away to join the Hunters in the darkness.

I swallowed. I had completely understood what she had said, but it made me realise just how hard my choice would be. The prophecy had confirmed my deepest fears.

Barely a second had passed since the clairvoyant had retreated, but to me, it felt like an eternity. All eyes were on me, so I forced a smile.

"Thank you, clairvoyant. I know what I must do now." No, I didn't know what I must do, but it seemed like the right thing to say, because the air got lighter after they heard my words.

"Normally, Hunters are not allowed to take sides. We are to observe and keep things neutral," Kensington said. "But the Great Dark Mage is a threat we cannot oversee. We may be neutral, but we are also children of nature, and nature sides the white mages."

I nodded, not knowing where he was taking this.

"That said I, Kensington of South Hunters Woods, the leader of the Hunters, will join you in the war." Kensington came and knelt in front of me. He raised his hands upwards and the trees parted above us to let the bright afternoon sunlight in.

"Wait!" I interjected quickly. "If you swear allegiance to me, you will be Bound! There will be no turning back from this Binding, and you will never be a Hunter again. You will no longer be the leader of South Hunters Woods, but a mage Bound to me. Are you willing?"

I had to give it to the guy. Kensington didn't blink nor hesitate. His 'aye' was firm and immediate. I shook my head at him.

"You can join the war even without being Bound," I said, and he understood that I was turning him down.

"Why?" he asked. There was no malice in his tone, just curiosity. He truly wanted to know.

"I . . ." I stopped. How do I tell him this? "We . . . don't have a bond," I said, and once the words left my mouth, I realised what the other Hunters would hear. They would know why Alpheus had left. I blushed right up to my roots.

"Oh," Kensington said knowingly.

"Uh . . ." damn my mouth. How does one do damage control for something like this?

"Yes, Crescentia is my mate." Alpheus affirmed, and my already red face burned brighter.

"Well, then how can we enter war while being neutral?" Kensington asked. He frowned and looked around at his fellow Hunters.

"You can, because you will be neutral if you are on my side," I said easily. "Nature will see to it, because the dark is out-balancing the white right now."

They knew that I was right and they all accepted my words as one.

"So, what do you want us to do?" Kensington asked me. "We have the same power as dark mages and white mages."

I smiled slowly, and they all took a step back again. It was my vampire smile.

"We are now heading to Rigs City to discuss. Kensington, you can come alone and brief the Hunters later," I said quickly. "We must move fast."

They nodded and the Hunters disappeared into the darkness, melting in as only those who were born to it could. Kensington came into the jeep with us. He sat at the back with the other three.

Alpheus's shoulders were less tense as he drove off.

Was that good? I asked him

Incredible, he replied. It was true. There were so many ways that 'talk' could go wrong.

Chapter 15

ONCE UPON A TIME

Whe drove over the bumpy road of South Hunters Woods in silence for about a minute before Kensington and Gwenwyn hit it off, much to all of our surprise. He started out asking her about her hair and he told her that he was fascinated with it. I understood his fascination, because I'd once been fascinated with it as well.

Her hair was really white, with just bare hints of blonde to keep it from being albino. She had in turn complimented his eyebrow and they went on to favourite stuff questions.

The rest of us just listened in, but they didn't seem to notice.

Suddenly, the road got smooth again and light flooded in. We all blinked hard against the sudden brightness. It felt like such a relief to see again.

The city that awaited us was a let-down after Royal City, but it was still something. The buildings were very . . . practical. There really were no other words for it. The buildings were packed close and low, like terrace houses. But as we drove on, we realised that it wasn't just that. That was just a housing area.

I instantly knew that this city had a power discrimination against the residents. The houses near the middle were grand, and amazing. I even saw four or five mansions.

"What is this?" I muttered. If I didn't know that this was Rigs City, I would never have believed that Nyhaivhar could change so much.

"They have a system now," Kensington said. "It depends on your lineage and also your job."

I raised my hand to stop him from saying anymore. I was bowled over in pain. The acute anxiety was punched into my heart, and my airway was closed, and I couldn't breathe.

Alpheus pulled over to the side of the road to let the other cars behind us pass. I was choking really badly. My hands were flailing around, slamming on the seat over and over.

Alpheus looked at me helplessly, his hands fluttering at his sides, knowing there was nothing he could do. This was terrible, the worst I've felt since forever. I tried to slam my body back on my seat repeatedly to get air through my throat, but it wasn't going to work because this wasn't natural; this was magical.

Finally, the anxiety left me and I took in big gulps of air. Bethamzar's presence was everywhere in this city. I slumped back into the seat and filled my lungs to the max.

"Go there," I said, pointing. Alpheus reached out to squeeze my knee in comfort before putting his hands on the wheel and pulling back into the road. He drove according to my directions, but I felt like we were going in circles. Everything was so new to me that I didn't know where was where, and all I could do was follow the pure presence.

Finally, we rounded at a shopping mall and I perked up. The place my mother enchanted was quite near. I pointed to the next right eagerly.

"Turn there."

As he turned to the right after the shopping mall, an amazing sight appeared before our eyes. Even Alpheus had to swerve to narrowly avoid another car because of the surprise.

In front of us was a wide open space, filled with growing plantation that seemed too peaceful and out-of-place in the middle of a busy, traffic-filled city. The entire place, not just the ground or plantation, glowed with bustling health. The brilliant vibration reached endlessly up to the skies and we couldn't help staring in awe.

Unconscious tears sprang into my eyes before I realised what was happening. My tears flowed because there, in the middle of all that gleaming life was the ancient, olden shack that used to be my village house.

"Oh," I said softly, as moisture filled my eyes and distorted my view. I blinked furiously, wanting to see it more than anything in the world. My mother's presence lingered there as if she'd never left. "As if her heart had never been torn out by my brother."

I felt shock in the jeep and was confused. Why were they shocked? And then I realised that I said the last line out loud. I hadn't told them my story yet, so this was shocking to them. I bit my lip.

"We have to go there. We absolutely must go there," I said steadily. I was proud that my voice didn't shake despite the turmoil in my heart. Alpheus's eyes flashed to my face, as if he knew what I was feeling and he turned into the next road to enter. The shack didn't just bring back good memories. I recalled Christopheri, my father, and wondered what happened there. I knew my mother would never

149

be with a Great Dark Mage, so he must have turned. Why would he turn, and what would that mean for me?

We parked at the side of the fence. I noticed that the area was completely fenced off and there was a sign that said "no trespassing". We walked along the fence until we found an opening, and there was a guy standing guard there.

He looked up with a serene expression as we drew near. He looked quite young, but judging from the white mage presence coming from his body, he wasn't. He raised a lazy finger and looked at us, sniffing the air. And then something about him clicked.

He had pale brown eyes. His eyes were so light that it was almost a mere reflection of colour. His light brown hair was tousled and messy, and he was dressed in a red shirt that hid under a black leather jacket and dark blue leather pants.

This was my mother's closest friend, Xinsutgen Al Nyhaivhar. He was Bound to her, but he wasn't anymore because she was dead. I could still sense that he was Bound, though. I guessed that staying in this place where her presence was so clear kept the Binding intact. He was notorious for using his nose to scent people.

"I smell a Great White Mage, four white mages, and a Hunter." He opened his eyes and sighed, looking away from us. "To what do I owe the pleasure of such a party?"

I looked at Alpheus and he nodded at me in encouragement. I took a deep breath a stepped forward.

"Xinsutgen," I said. We watched as he froze for five seconds. Slowly, he turned his head to look at me, his eyes growing wider with each passing moment.

"How do you know . . . ?" He whispered. He must not have recognised me yet.

"I am Crescentia Al Nyhaivhar." I said. I kept my eyes unswervingly n his face. "I am the daughter of Mordent Al Nyhaivhar, the Grand White Mage."

His eyes widened so far, I thought his eyeballs would fall out. He opened his mouth to say something but nothing came out. Instead, tears started rolling down his face. Somehow, seeing his tears was such a heart-breaking sight that I automatically went over to him and embraced him.

He cried for about three whole minutes on my shoulder and soaked my sleeve with his tears. I cringed internally, but it was no big deal, so I ignored it. There were more pressing matters to be addressed.

Once his tears dried up, he held my shoulders and looked into my eyes with his own piercingly pale brown ones. "Ah, yes. It is you. How could I have missed your presence?" he shook his head in shame.

I tapped his shoulder awkwardly, not quite sure how to comfort him. "It's fine; it's been more than many aeons since we last saw each other."

He gave me a rueful smile. "We haven't met since the beginning of time." I smiled at him, but I was rueful, too. That statement was the closest to the truth that I have ever known.

"I have come for one thing only," I said firmly, and I pointed towards my ancient house. I wasn't surprised that it was still standing properly. My mother's magic was powerful beyond the grave.

"We need to go inside to talk." I indicated towards my friends with my head. "They do not know anything yet."

He nodded in understanding. He knew that Bethamzar's name wasn't to be mentioned in this city, but in that sinewy house of light magic, it was safe to speak freely. He walked to the gate and took out a key from his pocket. I thought he was going to open it the normal way, but then I realised that the fence's gate had no keyhole.

He held the key in front of the gate and waited. There was a small burst of light from the key and it disintegrated into white glitter, shimmering before winking out of existence. The gate groaned twice before swinging open wide by itself easily.

He stepped aside to let us in. I looked at Alpheus who nodded at me, and then he looked at Ezra, who in turn looked at Quinteth, to Gwenwyn, to Kensington.

"Let's go." I swallowed a lump in my throat, and we went into the rabbit hole. *Hello, wonderland.*

Once we were all in my shack seated comfortably, I noticed just how old it all was. "Amazing," I breathed. It only just hit me that if I didn't die, I would be more than six hundred thousand years old. Now, I was just sixteen years old. It made me sad to think that my brilliant legacy was cut short by my own brother.

They were all looking at me expectantly. We were seated in a circle so that everyone could see everyone else. Xinsutgen was the only one not in the circle. He preferred to stand and lean against a wall to watch us. I got the feeling that he didn't trust us fully yet.

"So," I said, feeling a bit nervous. "Shall I start?"

Alpheus, who was sitting beside me, held my hand. "Yes."

"Start with 'once upon a time'," Gwenwyn blurted. I saw that some of them wanted to admonish her, but the fear in her eyes were unmistakable, so their chastisement died in their throats.

"This is no bedtime story," I warned. "This isn't *Cinderella*; this is a nightmare."

They kept their eyes in my face and I rolled my shoulders, getting my story straight in my head. "Once upon a time," I started, giving Gwenwyn a sad smile. "There was a Grand White Mage. She had a daughter and a son . . ."

I told them my deeply hidden past in great detail, only pausing for breath. The sky got darker as time passed. Once the story was told, we all sat in stunned silence.

Gwenwyn slumped onto the floor, breathing quietly in quick bursts of shock. Quinteth's face was frozen in horror. The guys were much better at controlling their emotions, but I could still feel that they were shaken.

Xinsutgen sighed. He was unmoved by my story because he had more or less known most of it. "So that was what had truly happened." He shook his head. "Bethamzar has to be stopped, but how?"

All of their eyes fell on me once more, but I had no solution to give, only more bad news.

"Bethamzar killing us is not the worst that could happen," I said slowly. I could feel their hope dissipating. This was too much for anyone to process in a day.

"What's the worst?" Xinsutgen asked gruffly. He truly felt like an uncle to me. "Don't hold anything back, Crescentia."

I bit my lip. "The worst is that if we die, or if I die, specifically, he could take my phoenix."

They looked at me.

"Why is that a bad thing?" Xinsutgen asked.

"Because I will never be able to be reincarnated again, but he can," I said, shivering. "Bethamzar plans to kill me and absorb the phoenix as I die. That will tip the balance of the scale of nature and catastrophe will be upon us." I shook my head feeling stressed.

They were silent again, pondering the depths of my words. They all looked too pale, except Alpheus. He squeezed my hand too hard and glared at me.

"You kept this all to yourself for all these years?" he was quietly enraged. He always hated it when I kept my burden to myself and didn't share it with him. "You should learn by now that we are not fragile! You *do not* have to carry the entire burden by yourself."

I nodded quickly and shook my hand, letting him know that he was hurting me. He lightened the pressure but didn't let go.

"I don't know how to defeat him," I admitted. "I know we have to remove the cursed blade first, otherwise we can't destroy him. But the blade has joined into his bloodstream as one." I frowned, furious that I couldn't find a way.

Xinsutgen tapped my back. "I think I know just the thing."

We all perked up, staring at him. He backed away for a moment and he looked up, thinking.

"Your mother kept a Book of Spells somewhere. She must have something that can help with it." He said slowly. "Do you know where she might have put it?"

"No," I said honestly. "She would never tell me something so important unless she thought I needed it."

Xinsutgen nodded, thinking. "That does sound like her. Well, it's alright, then. We will find another way."

I agreed. "Do you stay here?" I asked him.

"No, of course not," he shook his head. "There are too many memories here, I could never sleep. I have a house in the other district of the city." He looked at me wistfully. "It is one of the areas your mother purified."

I looked at the ground.

"We will stay here," I told him. "Can I have the key?"

He looked at me, frowning slightly. "Why?"

"It is my home," I said, surprised. "Of course I want to stay here."

He looked at me for a moment more, measuring my face for some emotion. Whatever it was, he sighed and held out his hand. Glitter shimmered into visible spectrum and became a solid key on his palm. He handed it over to me.

"I will take my leave now." He tipped his battered cap. "Have a good rest. I will be back tomorrow."

We nodded and waved goodbye. We watched as he left and we entered the old shack of a house again. We stared at each other in heavy silence. A cold wind blew and I shivered, noticing I wasn't the only one.

"Right, enough moping around," Quinteth clapped her hands. She had recovered quickly. As expected of the mature one. "Now, who's going to get the firewood?"

$$Chapter\ 16$$

STORY OF LIGHT AND SHADOW

We were up and about before dawn, laying things about to prepare for a Ritual.

"Are you sure we should do a cleansing Ritual now?" Ezra asked me for the third time. I could feel their doubts. I felt annoyance pervade throughout my body and I ground my teeth. Patience had never been my strong suit. My eyebrow twitched with the suppressed irritation.

"For the last time, yes, I'm sure," I snapped, throwing my hands up in exasperation. They backed away, and I felt guilty for saying it that way. I was just so edgy thinking about the war that was to come, because I was still clueless as to whether or not I would be able to make the right decision when the time came. We had sent Kensington away to warn the Hunters.

"Perhaps you should explain to them," Alpheus murmured in my ear as he passed me, carrying sage to lay on the ground on my right.

"I'm doing this as preparation for war. The cleaner the city, the better chance we have of winning." I sucked in a breath and smiled at them in apology. "Sorry I'm being such a grouch."

They all smiled at me in relief that that was all it was, and went to work with more enthusiasm. This made me aware that I had to keep my emotions in check. I suppressed a sigh. This meant more suppressed emotion. It's a wonder I haven't had a heart attack from stress.

We were ready for the Ritual just as dawn approached. I closed my eyes to absorb its rays for a moment, and then I quickly drew the pentagram on the ground and stepped into it.

"*Light!*" I commanded, and the candles surrounding us flared up in pale purple flames. My friends stood around the pentagram in their usual order. I picked up the sage from the ground and put it in Alpheus's candle's flames and move on to Gwenwyn, going in a full circle.

"*White sage of white mage, white of light and white of might,*" my voice rang out with pure power. The entire area seemed to absorb my words and I felt another presence standing at the edge of our circle. Melancholic feelings filled my heart and I smiled. My mother was here. "*Keep the pure and evil purge, white of might bring tide of white.*" I could feel my mother chanting along with me.

The dawn's rays were absorbed into the circle and the pentagram beneath my feet shone with the brilliant orange hues. The pureness of the start of a new day was empowering the circle's magic.

I raised my palms to the sky and closed my eyes. I allowed myself to be the liaison of power flowing from the sky to the ground, making a magical bridge. I focused on the rosemary on the ground and it appeared in my palm. I went to Alpheus's candle again.

"*Bitter herb of white mage, cleanse the spite of netherworld.*" I walked around the circle, burning the rosemary until it was completely consumed by purple flames. *"Might of white be kept divine, dark of night be kept concealed."* The flames were not hot, and I watched as the rosemary disappeared into purple light before vanishing into the power.

I picked up the final ingredient. It was lavender, my trademark. My mother had asked me to choose before, which herb I wanted as my trademark. I had asked her why I needed a trademark, and she told me it would make my powers more specific and concentrated.

I turned towards my mother's presence and smiled while holding the lavender. I could tell she was remembering as well. She had asked me why I wanted lavender.

"I like the smell, and it is relaxing. Also, it reminds me of you," My ancient fourteen year old self had told her, and she smiled with delight, the way she was smiling at me now.

I burnt it on Alpheus's candle again. *"Pure of colour and white of power,"* I chanted, and the power around us flared up with potency. I moved on to Gwenwyn. *"Light of light and raise the power."* I moved on to Quinteth. *"Dark cries unheard as light consumes."* I stopped in front of Ezra. *"To light the power and might of white."*

My mother's pride in me was felt throughout the circle. My friends noticed because their eyes widened and they looked at me, smiles of wonder on their faces. Our eyes glowed with the same deep blood red that came from using power and connected us.

"Release!" I proclaimed.

The great power that had been building in our circle blasted outwards, and it felt like a magical earthquake. Only those with the power would be able to feel it. Even though we're on the ground, nothing bad would happen, because we were in a place of Old Magic. In those times, one could draw pentagrams in the air and chant anywhere.

We all stood firm in our circle, letting the spell absorb our power to cleanse the land. I felt all traces of dark mages become purified and the hardened and evil hearts of the people in Rigs City became light as grudges were released. It cleansed and cleansed until it reached one area where the power bounced back every time it tried to purify it.

It was the Hollow. I tried to push my power out harder, but a feathery touch on my shoulder stopped me. I looked up to see my mother shake her head once, and disappeared.

The entire city had been cleansed except the Hollow, and as much as I wanted to cleanse that place, it was impossible. The dark magic there was too great; I would have to personally go. I gritted my teeth and ended the spell.

The purple flames went out all at once.

"It is finished. Thank you," I said, and stepped out of the pentagram. It stopped glowing and disintegrated. This time, I was thanking more than nature. I was also thanking my mother.

My mother's presence no longer lingered, but was felt throughout the area.

"She was here, wasn't she?" Quinteth said in awe. I smiled at them. Our eye were no longer glowing a brilliant red; they were back to normal.

"She sure was," I replied and a gentle warm breeze blew.

The others went back to the shack first and I sat on the grass with Alpheus at my side. We were silent for a while. I got up and pushed him down on the ground gently and kneeled over him.

"What's wrong, Crescentia?" he asked quietly. He didn't stop me from doing whatever I wanted with him. He always let me have my way with him because he gave his life and body to me in every way possible. I ran my hands over his chest leaned down so that our faces were parallel.

"I love you," I whispered, and the fear that I had been suppressing seeped into my words. I was terrified of the possibility losing him in the war later. He was my only life. He closed his eyes in understanding and he reached for me and pulled me down on him.

"As I love you," he whispered in my ear, and he rolled me over so that I was pinned to the ground. He pressed his lips to mine and I opened my mouth, giving access to his tongue. He obliged and slipped his tongue into my mouth and our tongues twisted together. I moaned and writhed below him and raised my hips to his and he pressed himself into me. I arched my chest to him and he groaned and kissed me harder and more savagely. I held his shirt and pulled it over his head and marvelled at his smooth chest and abs. More clothes joined his shirt on the ground. For the first time since I was reincarnated, I became truly one with Alpheus again.

It was a long time before we were back in the old shack and eating cereal. I felt a presence at the gate. It was Xinsutgen. His presence lingered there and I felt his patience.

"Come in," I said. I honestly didn't need the key. This place was as much mine as my mother's, since I was born in it. The magical fence gate obeyed my words and let him in. I wondered if the place would obey Bethamzar as well. It probably would, but he wouldn't be able to come in without being purified.

Xinsutgen came in and walked towards the shack. I really wanted to call it a house, but it was really nothing more than a shack. Nobody had heard of architecture back then.

"Good morning," he greeted us as he came in and sat on the floor. "You're up early."

I nodded. "We performed a dawn cleansing."

"Ah," he smiled wistfully. "I haven't performed a circle Ritual since . . ." he trailed off.

"Since my mother died," I said easily. "She's still around, though. She joined us in the cleansing."

Xinsutgen's face filled with wistful longing. "I wished I'd been here to see that."

"Haven't you seen her in your dream yesterday?" I asked, surprised.

He looked at me, equally surprised. "How do you know?"

"The same way I know she was here with us." The sentence sounded abstract, even to me. But I had no idea how else to put it.

He smiled at me. "That's refreshing. The power in you is very well favoured by nature." He laughed. "Your mother chose well."

I looked down. "But it's my fault that Bethamzar is the way he is."

Xinsutgen came to me and held my hands, looking at me straight in the eyes. "Yes, it is your fault, but not in the way you think."

My friends' indignant silent protests filled the air, but he ignored it like it wasn't there.

"Without light, there can be no shadow. Without shadow, there can be no light," He told me. "If you were to be accepted into the power, someone has to be the shadow to your light. It just so happens that Bethamzar was powerful enough to be considered your shadow." He stared into my eyes with his pale brown ones, trying to tell me something.

I nodded my understanding. He was telling me that even without the jealousy that led Bethamzar to this, it would have happened anyway, but maybe in a different way. This was the balance of nature.

"So if I defeat him, who will be the shadow?" I asked.

Xinsutgen shook his head fast. "There will only ever be one shadow. I have come to terms with this idea, but as much as it pains me to say it, it must be said." He took a breath. "We need to get rid of your mother's lingering presence. Once the shadow and light are gone, you will be fine. This is probably confusing, but it will balance the nature scale."

I nodded. It *was* confusing, but I knew with all my heart that what he said was true. I didn't know if I was ready for it yet, though. The last time, it was my brother who killed our mother. This time, I have to get rid of my mother and my brother. My shoulders hunched with the weight of my burden.

There was another thing I wanted to ask Xinsutgen, but I wasn't sure if I could ask about it in my circle's presence, so I got up and went to the door and motioned for him to come along. Alpheus got up to follow, but I shook my head gently at him. I was sure that this was something that was a bit too personal.

I'll just be a minute, I assured him, and left to the fields with Xinsutgen. I subconsciously brought him to the place where I had been *with* Alpheus earlier and blushed slightly, remembering how it had felt.

"What is it?" Xinsutgen was looking at me curiously. I cleared my throat, and then tried to focus on my task at hand.

"I wanted to know about . . . about Christopheri." I bit my lip. I still found it hard to think of Christopheri as my *father*. I looked at Xinsutgen pleadingly. "Had he always been a dark mage, or did he turn?"

Xinsutgen stared at me, contemplating whether to tell me the truth. I looked right back at him earnestly.

He sighed. "I don't really know much. It has something to do with your grandmother, the Original Mage, and a prophecy." He saw the confusion on my face, and he scrunched his own, thinking hard. "When the Original Mage started dabbling in magic and spells, her first prophecy ever was about fulfilling the Will of the Garden of Eden, or something of the sort. She had prophesized that one of her descendants will be the one who bore the symbol of the phoenix, and one who will bear the symbol of the dragon."

"This is where the famous prophecy came from," he kicked at a stone and then sat down on the grass. I followed suit since it didn't seem like it was going to be a short story. *"The tail of the dragon shall impale the phoenix which, in turn, rises from the ashes.* The rest of the prophecy was lost with time, apparently, the dragon and the phoenix would wage war against each other. If the dragon won this war, there was no more hope for humankind. But if the phoenix won the war . . ." he trailed off, frowning. He couldn't seem to recall much of the ancient context. "It has something to do with the Forbidden Fruit and the Garden of Eden," he finished, looking more than a bit chagrined to be unable to remember.

We were silent for a moment while I digested this new bit of info. I rolled my eyes at him.

"You still didn't tell me about Christopheri," I reminded him, successfully keeping the exasperation out of my voice. He blinked and chuckled.

"I didn't, did I?" he sighed. "I'm actually sketchy about the details. I think it was arranged by your grandmother so that your mother would bear you and Bethamzar." Xinsutgen scratched his head. "He was probably turned by nature to be your mother's counterpart as shadow."

"Oh." It felt like all the wind in my chest left my feeling breathless. So that was why I had to grow up not knowing that my father was my father? It didn't seem like a good enough reason. It just didn't seem right that I was on the side of nature whilst it endlessly ruined the lives of my loved ones, just so it could keep its precious balance.

"Okay," I murmured, and got up to go back into the hut. Xinsutgen politely declined my offer to help him stand, telling me that he wanted to rest for a little while more.

Well, time to get back to Alpheus.

Chapter 17

WAR OF THE MAGES

We left the the shack around eleven to set off for the Hollow. Each of us carried a small bag of spell ingredients with us. We set off on foot, leaving the jeep behind. As we walked, I mulled over the many events of the past month.

It was hard to believe that just about two months ago, I was Wendy Elise Fletcher, and my biggest worry was keeping good grades, thinking up good choreography and wondering if Mark liked me, too. It felt like an entire lifetime ago.

I was hit by the irony of the last sentence. I had an entire past that was mine but wasn't. I wasn't sure if Wendy existed in me anymore. I felt like I was more than eighty per cent Crescentia, but I would never be Crescentia again, except in name and in power. I touched Mark's necklace. It now represented more than just our relationship; it represented my life as Wendy.

"Do you have any idea how you are going to destroy them both?" Xinsutgen asked, coming up to my left.

"I don't know," I replied bluntly.

We probably looked like tourists to the residents of Rigs City. We walked around admiring the self-sustained city. We saw that they used hydroelectric generators. I remembered that it rained constantly in the southern part of the Regions. No wonder they were so well sustained.

As we walked on, the dark presences grew stronger. Even though we'd performed such a powerful dawn cleansing Ritual, the dark came back too fast. There must be quite a gathering of dark mages. I tried not to think about Bethamzar being in the midst of them, but the image ate away any other thought I was having.

It was especially hard to forget because his presence was to most potent one of all. Even my friends were unconsciously scrunching their noses. They still looked around like they didn't notice it, but their noses twitched. Alpheus had noticed, though. He was Alpheus, after all.

He looked at me and I nodded my confirmation. His face went into poker mode. I smiled at him and rolled my eyes.

It's totally fine for you to look grim, I told him.

Not if it brings fear to the others, he replied.

I smiled and looked at them ruefully. They were admiring the city, but underneath it all, they were plenty scared. We were going into war, after all. The chances of us losing our lives were so great that we had to choose to look away, or we wouldn't be able to move.

I don't think it will make a difference, I responded sadly. It was my fault, after all. If I hadn't Bound them to me, they wouldn't be compelled to follow me. Scratch that. If I hadn't hesitated at the last moment all those years ago, Bethamzar wouldn't be alive now.

I frowned, a thought occurring to me. This was all in the best interest of nature. Just to keep the scale balanced, sweet and caring Bethamzar had to be turned. Was this the justice that I had been protecting all this while? How many more mages were turned just to be the shadow of another white mage? Was Christopheri turned as well, for the sake of turning Bethamzar?

I felt sick. Then all this time, I was just being used as a tool to keep the balance of the scale, even though the scale wouldn't have tipped in the first place? Was that what I existed for? My sinking feeling grew. So what did my mother die for? Was she used to fulfil Bethamzar's shadow to my light?

I was a phoenix. I was never going to die permanently, so what did this mean for me?

"The tail of the dragon shall impale the phoenix which, in turn, will rise from the ashes."

That has already happened. His magic had forced me into death for the first time.

"The rise of the phoenix shall bring great power upon the dragon."

That meant that Bethamzar would be able to use my phoenix, but for what?

"The phoenix shall make a choice, but one may not be raised again."

I bit my lip. This was the part that I was worried about the most. When the time came, I would have to make an important choice, but I didn't know which choice it was yet. If I made the wrong choice and died, I wasn't going to be reincarnated again. Bethamzar would take my phoenix.

We were close now. I could taste the bitter air. Despite the now-afternoon sun, there was a place ahead of us that was plunged into darkness. There was no light there. It was a force field. To humans, that place would simply not exist.

We stopped a few feet from the force field. Xinsutgen groaned. Our eyes went to his face.

"It's alright, I'm fine." He huffed. "I just can't believe this is happening. Especially because the child is the one in the midst of all this." he waved his hand at the dark force field. The force field looked like a dome with black water rolling down from the top.

I nodded. "We have to move now."

We all held hands and took deep breaths. I squeezed some power out through my hands and made it flow through them, strengthening them. They closed their eyes and focused, letting the power settle into them.

As one, we stepped into the force field.

"Hello, welcome everybody," a sharp rasping voice greeted us. We opened our eyes quickly. There was a line of ugly dark mages in front of us. They were all in a fighting stance; as if ready to defend any attack we might throw against them.

The dark mage who spoke was in front of them. There was a silent moment of standstill. Then the silence ended explosively. Both sides charged forward, and hands were blurry as pentagrams were casted at high speeds.

I drew six pentagrams within three seconds, using both my hands. I casted them into the dark mages while calling out the words of power. Six mages fell and writhed on the floor. They were only temporarily inconvenienced, but temporary was long enough for me to Bind them.

Their magic was drained away and they were pulled into the earth by the pentagrams. I didn't have time to pause as more took their place. We were outstandingly outnumbered. The pentagrams were not enough. It was time for some Old Magic.

I waved away nine pentagrams that were thrown at me by coating my hand with power. They must have been specifically ordered to target me. More pentagrams were thrown at me and I dodged, waving them away quickly.

I heard a gasp and saw two pentagrams fly towards Quinteth. She was too slow in countering them and I quickly waved at them. I raised my power so that any pentagram I targeted would disintegrate. The rest of them were doing well in attacking and countering. Unfortunately, only Xinsutgen and I could cast the Binding spells. So I had to quickly Bind all the dark mages they left writhing on the ground.

"I'll do this!" Xinsutgen yelled at me. With a single stroke of his arm, seven pentagrams sprung forth and instantly Bound a dark mage. He kept up his strokes and he chanted the spells endlessly.

I ran forward through the throngs of mages, determined to get to the one that mattered. I was hit by a stray pentagram. It clung around my arm and clamped hard. My bone broke and I screamed. My power instantly healed me and purged the dark pentagram from my arm.

I waved away more pentagrams. Our group slowly progressed forward. This wasn't good. If we took out one, three more took their place. It almost felt like we were the Japanese and they were the Chinese in the war. There were so many of them.

I tried to copy what Xinsutgen was doing. I felt a guiding hand and knew my mother was here, too. For a moment, I was filled with hope before something clicked.

"The rise of the phoenix shall bring great power upon the dragon."

It wasn't about me all along. It was my mother. Bethamzar could use my phoenix to resurrect her and raise her into darkness. If he raised the Grand White Mage into darkness, then all would be lost. So this was why he couldn't do anything even though I'd died. He couldn't get my phoenix from far away and needed me here personally to lure our mother in.

"Go away!" I pleaded. She understood in a split second, but it was a split second too late. Her presence was ripped away from me, and a loud cackle filled the air. The other mages cackled along with it, and I was dismayed to feel their power grow. They turned their glowing red eyes on me.

"Crescentia!" Alpheus shouted, shocking me out of my reverie. He waved away the pentagrams hurled at me. I shook my head to get a hold of myself. Now was not the time to be stunned.

I raised my hands, palms outwards. I focused on the white sage in my small pouch bag. It appeared in front of my palms, floating in the air.

"*Light!*" I cried. The sage flared up in brilliant purple flames and blasted many of them backwards. My Old Magic wasn't made to Bind, it was made to purify. Purifying them was to end their life. I used to have qualms about it, but in this moment, I didn't have time to Bind every last one of them. I focused on the mages that were hit.

There were perhaps forty that were caught in the purple flames. I slammed my palms together and threw power into the spell. A brilliant light shone from my closed palms and there were screams from the dark mages and they exploded in light.

This spell was going to drain me like hell, because it wouldn't just stop there. The other mages that were caught in the explosion were bursting into the bright flames as well. It was a chain reaction, and it would draw on my power until every last one had cleared.

I tried to think. I needed my power. Going against Bethamzar with just the power I had on reserve was like suicide. I closed off the spell. I had destroyed perhaps two hundred dark mages. The number was frightening. Just how many were there? Two hundred wasn't enough, but it would have to do.

We advanced forward quickly, not wasting the opening I had created. We ran and ran, fighting as we went. Another wave of mages came upon us. I imagined all the seven Binding pentagrams in my mind and gave a quick slash in the air with my hand. The slash was coated with power, and the seven pentagrams materialised all at once.

Xinsutgen nodded in approval before turning back to fight. I shoved the seven pentagrams at a dark mage, the words of power spilling from my lips. I had no time to enjoy watching the power get stripped from him and I slashed the air again, calling forth the next seven pentagrams.

I called out the words at high speeds, slashing the air endlessly, using both hands. The dark mages were dwindling, but so was my power and energy. Another loud cackle filled the air and I felt my mother's distress. I realised with a jolt that she was with Bethamzar.

We all fought harder. It seemed like an endless battle as wave after wave came forward. It could have been minutes since we came, or it could have been hours.

My eyes were glowing red. Where was he?

"Xinsutgen, purify them!" I shouted at him. I waved away three pentagrams thrown at me. He understood what I was saying. I couldn't waste my power on the small fries. He had to clear them off.

Without hesitation, he jerked back and threw sage into the air and blasted it into dark blue flames. It burst forward and smashed into a great wave of the mages. They all burst into flames. He kept his palms together, keeping the light glowing. The resulting chain reactions were spectacular.

However, as old as he was, Xinsutgen wasn't a Great White Sorcerer. His magic only lasted for a few minutes before he was brought to his knees. His forehead beaded with sweat and the strain of it was set onto his brow.

I realised too late that we came unprepared. This wasn't a battle we could win, much less a war. Just as I was about to give the order to retreat, we heard something like a stampede. Time seemed to stop as all our attention were directed behind us, at the force field. I wanted to jump for joy.

The Hunters were here.

We cheered and were joined quickly. The amount of Hunters was astonishing. I could almost say that we were no longer outnumbered. They went forward led by Kensington who winked at Gwenwyn before smiling at Alpheus.

"We're not the only ones!" He called and dove into the magical brawl.

Alpheus was surprised for a moment and then understood as the North Hunters sprang forward as well. They greeted him and me quickly and warmly before joining the fray. I felt more and more confident with each addition to our side. This was it. It was all or nothing now.

We charged.

I didn't use any power. It made me feel like a coward, but I couldn't help it. I had to save every last drop of magic I had for Bethamzar. I stood behind Alpheus's protection as he advanced forward with the North Hunters. We were making great time as we more or less ran through the openings made for us by our comrades.

I focused all my senses into searching out Bethamzar. His presence was thickest at the hollow tree where he had turned. I pointed mutely and he moved quickly without question. I looked behind us at the chaos. I caught my friends' eyes and motioned them forward. I needed my circle with me.

They broke away instantly, leaving the battle to Xinsutgen and the Hunters. They hurried to catch up with us.

We stopped at the hollow. Bethamzar emerged from the tree, and we all simultaneously stepped back. Bethamzar put a whole new level to ugly. Although his skin was dark grey and brown and there were ugly criss-cross patterns scrawled across his balding head and face, I could still tell that it was my beloved brother.

No, wait. He wasn't beloved anymore. He was a creature of the dark, right?

In his hands, he held a crystal ball. Inside the ball, was my mother's presence. In other words, it was her soul.

Bethamzar's eyes cut directly to me, as if nobody else stood between us. He smiled.

"Well, sister, how nice to see you again." The black smoke from his mouth filled the air with foulness, and Quinteth and Gwenwyn gagged. I felt nauseous as well. "Guess what? I hate nice."

I stepped around Alpheus. "Don't do this, Bethamzar," I tried. This was still my brother, dark mage or not. I had to try.

He laughed. "I think not." He waved his hand at me and I was thrown backwards into another tree. My back slammed hard and my head snapped back. The wind was completely knocked out of me and I gasped.

"Do you remember those words, sister?" he cackled as my friends threw pentagrams at him, waving the crystal ball around. "Those were the last words you ever said to me." He waved at my friends absently, sending them flying into other trees. Their pentagrams disintegrated uselessly.

There was no reasoning with him. The Bethamzar I knew was dead now; murdered by Christopheri and cursed with a blade. I closed my eyes, feeling a part of me die off with my ancient family. It was a part of me that I should have released a long time ago.

When I opened my eyes, they shone with new resolve. Bethamzar noticed and sneered.

"Come on, then, sister. Hit me with your best shot!" he threw his head back and howled, and the tree I was bracing myself on started to fall on top of me. I quickly ran out from underneath before I could get smashed completely.

I remembered my mother's book of spells. I focused on that one spell I had to cast, making it form in my mind. It was the one spell that my mother had taught me from her book, because according to her, it was for emergencies.

If this wasn't an emergency, I didn't know what was.

Bethamzar drew a pentagram and threw it at me. I coated my hand with power and tried to wave it away, but it merely moved and slammed into me. I lost the ability to move my own body. The pentagram kept me locked in its grip. Alpheus threw himself forward and drew a pentagram in the air. I was surprised. Was he powerful enough to do that?

Lend me your strength! Alpheus's voice burst into my head. I understood and shoved my power to towards him. I was hit with a sense of de já vu. This had happened before.

Alpheus's power was boosted. He channelled my power into the pentagram and threw it towards Bethamzar. I think we were all shocked when Bethamzar was blasted backwards. Well, it was Alpheus, after all.

Bethamzar growled, annoyed as he shoved himself back up. He kept his grip on the crystal ball firm. "Stay out of this!" he drew a pentagram. I recognized that pentagram and was filled with horror. I somehow managed to make my power burst outwards and released myself from my pentagram and I was about to hurl myself in front of Alpheus when something else clicked.

Time slowed as my brain went into hyper overdrive. That pentagram was meant to kill. If I saved Alpheus, I would die. If I died here, Bethamzar could get his hands on my phoenix. My body was frozen as my eyes watched the pentagram float slowly towards Alpheus. Alpheus was trying to wave it away but his power was no match for Bethamzar's.

I couldn't let him die, but I couldn't die either. This was my choice. It wasn't me who may not live, it was Alpheus. And that was completely unacceptable. It all came down to one thing. The crystal ball. I raised both my hands and called forth a giant wave of power from within me.

My left hand faced the pentagram and my right hand faced the crystal ball. *"Release!"* I bellowed. My power exploded outwards from my palms. It destroyed the pentagram at the same time threw the crystal ball out of his hands. Tears of sorrow ran down my face. *Goodbye, mother.* I opened my palm to the crystal ball, ready to destroy it.

Bethamzar's hand was caught in the power and he howled in rage. "Enough!" he raised his hands and someone else stepped out of the Hollow and took place in front of him. My hands froze and I was appalled. It was Mark. Bethamzar's consciousness must have been Shielding as he followed us and he must have found out about Mark.

"Mark!" I shrieked in fear. In his hands, he held a cursed blade. His eyes were glowing red and unfocused and I realised that Bethamzar had possessed him. Bethamzar kept his eyes closed in concentration as he focused on moving his puppet. My friends struggled to help but Bethamzar threw pentagrams at them and kept their bodies locked, the way mine was just now.

My mind was swirling with different mixed feelings as I watched Mark advance towards me jerkily. I saw Bethamzar's brow crease and sweat broke out over his rotten skin. Ah, jackpot. Doing all this must really be draining his power. He was also still feeding power to the dark mages.

Mark stopped in front of me, hands raised, blade poised in the air. "Be gone, sister." Bethamzar's words spilled from Mark's mouth. The cursed blade cut through the air, aiming straight for my heart. Right before it hit, I recovered and gave Bethamzar my best vampire smile.

"After you, brother."

I waved my arms out and the blade was thrown backwards, flying out of Mark's hands and straight towards Bethamzar. Mark's body shuddered violently and collapsed on the ground, unconscious. The blade had very little damage on Bethamzar. It just stunned him for moment, but a moment was all I needed.

I drew on my friends' power. My circle was here, and I was ready. I threw all my power into my hands as I drew the purifying pentagram. This time wasn't going to be like the last. This time it wasn't just a purifying spell, and this time, I had people to protect. I had Alpheus to protect.

The magnificent light exploded from the pentagram. I ran forward, Shielding myself from his Sight. He frantically tried to wave the pentagram away and I saw relief on his ugly face when it dissipated. I gritted my teeth and Unshielded right in front of him.

His eyes widened in understanding. The purification spell was just a distraction. I was never going to replay the past. I punched my right hand through his chest and released the spell into his body. It was the spell that I put every last drop of magic we all had into.

It was the spell from my mother's book of spells. It was a spell to get rid of and purify cursed items. I locked eyes with my brother one last time. I saw it there again, in his eyes. I saw the young, cheeky Bethamzar who always stood up for me and never left me behind. I was doing the only thing I could do for that young Bethamzar. I was returning him to himself.

"No!" he shrieked as the spell took place and my hand was repulsed out of his chest and I was thrown backwards again and slammed onto the ground beside Mark. I spit grass out of my mouth. He was carried into the air. I called on all the magic in the air and sent it towards him, strengthening the spell. My great magic was flowing through his body.

The tiny shards of the Dragon Blade and the other blade in his veins were seized and shook as the spell released it from its curse. As the shards were microscopic and spread throughout his body, it purified him at the same time. I watched as he shone through every pore with a blinding pale purple light. His eyes were thrown open wide and the light shone dazzlingly out of him.

His ugliness was stripped away from him and he looked like the Bethamzar I knew and loved. He burst into flames of light and his body was eaten away. As the light dimmed, I saw my beloved brother stand beside my mother and they smiled at each other before smiling at me.

"Goodbye," I whispered. They disappeared, and then everything turned dark and I breathlessly felt my head hit the ground.

Chapter 18

NORMAL AGAIN . . . KIND OF

I opened my eyes slowly. My eyelids seemed too heavy, like they were glued closed for too long. When my vision cleared from the blurriness, I saw that I was in a white room and there was an IV drip stuck in my left wrist. Ugh, that must mean I was in a hospital. As my senses came back to me, I wrinkled my nose. Yeah, I was in a hospital. I slowly looked around without moving my head. Something told me that moving my head wasn't the best idea right now.

I saw heads.

Don't worry, the heads were attached to bodies, and the bodies were attached to my parents. When I stirred, Alex felt the movement and looked up blearily. When he saw that I was awake, his left hand shot out and shook my mother, keeping his eyes trained on my face.

Adrienne was alert instantly, having been roughly awakened by my tactless dad. Her eyes immediately went to my face. She stood up slowly, trying not to startle me. I wanted to roll my eyes.

"Hey guys," I croaked. "What happened to me?"

Alex patted my arm. "You had an epileptic fit. It was the grand mal seizure. You were at the top of the stairs when you had it."

I was surprised. "I have epilepsy?"

Adrienne patted my arm reassuringly. "It's fine. You only had it once before. The doctors said it's only a big deal if it happens consistently. We watched over you but you didn't get any more fits, so we didn't tell you."

I went "Oh," and stayed still. I felt like I was forgetting something important. "What was I doing at the top of the stairs?"

"You were carrying your bags to your room, remember?" Alex said, looking worried. "We just came back from a trip to Queenstown, remember?"

I nodded. "Oh, yeah." I didn't remember anything of the sort. I only vaguely remembered saying goodbye to a lot of people in the school gym. Why was I saying goodbye in a school gym? I was puzzled.

Remora came whirling in like a strawberry blonde hurricane.

"You crazy girl!" she lurched forward and grabbed both my hands. "I'm so glad you're okay!" there were unshed tears in her eyes. I hung on to her hands, feeling supremely grateful that I could. I thought I would never see her again. Then I frowned. Why wouldn't I ever see her again?

"So am I, Reams." I used my childhood nickname for her. She laughed and hugged me lightly, cautious of the IV drip and pulled back.

I looked around at them all and smiled contentedly. This was more or less everything I needed in life. There was a small pinch in my chest, as if I was missing someone without knowing who. I banished the thought. Right now, the people in front of me were the most important ones.

Weren't they?

"Where's Mark?" I wondered aloud. I was surprised that he wasn't here.

"He's resting at home, I think. He was at the bottom of the stairs and you fell on him," Alex replied.

I sat up and my head felt like it snapped backwards. The whole room swirled around and Alex rushed forward to lay my head back down gently on the pillow. I felt kind of nauseous.

"Be careful, you fell quite a long way," Alex warned me.

"You scared the living daylights out of us, what with the loud banging." Adrienne put her hand over her heart. "The doctor said you'll be having a major concussion." She paused, shaking her head. "He said it was a miracle that you two didn't break anything."

"So when can I be discharged?" I said brightly. Remora laughed in her carefree way.

Remora nudged my arm, and I suppressed an urge to moan in pain. "That's my girl." She laughed in relief as tears of joy made tear tracks down her face.

Adrienne put her hands on my arm. "That's our girl," she corrected.

We were filled with sweetness then, and I had a quaint feeling of closure. We started chatting and catching up. It was obvious to them that I didn't remember much of the last two months, so they filled me in. Whatever they told me felt oddly out of place, but I was content to settle for it.

There was a sound of shuffling feet and Mark's head popped in.

"Hey, she's awake!" He came in and I saw that he was using crutches. Yikes, that was probably my fault. Alex pulled a chair over to the bed and Mark nodded his thanks before sitting down. He looked at me tenderly. I lightly raised my hand to touch his cheek, feeling deeply grateful that he was alright. "It's just a deep sprain." He turned his cheek to kiss my palm.

I shared a connected look with Mark and we smiled.

"I thought you were supposed to be resting at home?" I asked him.

He reached out and touched the necklace around my neck. "That was the idea." He grinned at me.

Suddenly, I heard a voice in my head.

I'll wait for you forever, it said. It was a guy's voice, and it felt oddly familiar. A wave of nostalgia filled me when I heard it, and I had the strange impression that home was wherever that guy was. But who was he?

I frowned in confusion. There was a brief, blurry flash of a guy's face in my mind, and my breath caught. The guy was incredibly beautiful.

"What's wrong?" Mark asked me, gently smoothing my hair back from my face. I shook my head, shoving my crappy thoughts away.

"Everything is just right." I touched his face and smiled.

Epilogue

THROUGH HIS EYES

"A re you sure this was a good idea?" Gwenwyn asked me for the eighth time as we watched Crescentia . . . no, Wendy reunites with her family. They watched her longingly. I could tell they didn't like sharing her with the humans. Gwenwyn was gnawing on her thumbnail.

"It has already been done," I said calmly, even if the surge of turmoil that wreaked havoc in my chest was anything but. I took a slow, quiet breath as she shared another loving look with the human boy. I felt like there was a sharp knife slicing my heart slowly. I had to take it like a man. This was the closure that she had craved.

"She doesn't need them," Ezra grumbled. "I can't believe it worked in the first place."

Quinteth scowled at the strawberry blonde girl. "That girl is so possessive, it's irritating." We watched as the blonde grabbed Wendy's hands. It was so odd to think of my beloved as two different people at once.

I sighed. "There's no point in us watching her from here. We should go and find a permanent residence somewhere, and perhaps find some work." I thought about our meagre funds and suppressed a cringe. "We should prepare for the day she remembers and comes to live with us again."

They gave the window one more longing look before tearing their eyes away.

"At least she's alive this time," Ezra said with relief evident in his voice.

Gwenwyn rolled her eyes at him, and then turned to me. "Alpheus, what made you think of this?"

I thought of the best way to respond, and then I realised that there wasn't a best way, there was just an honest way. "She thought about them a lot," I responded. "When we were going towards the Hollow, she thought about them. Before we left Queenstown, she swore that she would be Wendy to her parents once this was all over."

I closed my eyes and shrugged. "I was indulging her wishes." They were quiet for a while. I would miss her a lot, but at least I knew where she was and could visit her whenever I wanted. I thought back to the moment when we were at the Hollow.

*   *   *

When Crescentia fell unconscious on the ground at the Hollow, I was speared to the ground with fear. My eyes clung to her, waiting for signs of life. There weren't any, and I was frozen. My mind was blank, and white noise filled my ears.

Gwenwyn lurched forward once the pentagram released us and staggered towards Crescentia. The sight made me crawl to my feet as well, and I staggered over to her, ignoring the swaying in my legs. Her long black hair was splayed out around her body and the sight made my heart ache in fear.

Once Quinteth and Ezra were freed, they fell into each other's' arms for a few minutes before looking after the human boy and they tried to heal him with whatever mediocre power they had left.

I knelt by her side and picked her up and turned her around, shaking her slightly. "Crescentia, answer me. Crescentia?" I called. My heart stopped. She wasn't breathing. I laid her down again and pulled her jaw down.

I pressed my lips to hers and blew air into her lungs. I injected some of the little power I had left into her. I felt her chest rise in response and I pulled back and watched as she coughed and she breathed on her own. Her eyes fluttered open slightly, but I doubted she could see anything.

Her eyes held a blank look that I saw in blind people's eyes. "Alpheus?" she barely whispered it, her hand rose weakly at her side, searching for me. I hung on to her hand, feeling my life return to me.

"You're eyes are orange-green now," I told her softly, feeling tears gather at the rims of my eyes and spilling over. Her eyes were a glorious colour of sunrise and green grass. A weak smile lifted her lips.

"Is it now?" she breathed. I could tell she wasn't really in the present. This was almost a state of sleeping-while-awake.

"Yes, it is." I felt her consciousness give way and her eyes rolled back into her head and she went limp in my arms.

"She won't be waking up any time soon." Xinsutgen ran up to us, panting. "She threw everything she had into that spell. It could be days, weeks maybe." He sank to the ground and nodded at us all. "It's over. The battle and the war are over. The risen phoenix can live. However, we lost about fifty or so Hunters in the battle."

Gwenwyn's head snapped up and there was fear in her eyes. "Kensington?" she breathed desperately. Xinsutgen pressed his lips together, and then blew out air.

"If you have any power left to heal him, now is the time," Xinsutgen told her sadly. She gasped and blood drained out of her face. She patted my shoulder, telling me to look after Crescentia and she darted into the field, searching for Kensington.

I held her to me with shaking hands. My precious girl had been taken from me once; I couldn't allow it to ever happen again. I was also shaken to hear that so many of our comrades had fallen. I put my head on her shoulder, breathing in the scent from her hair. She always smelt of fresh lavenders, her trademark flower. She loved that colour.

"My life belongs to you, Crescentia," I whispered into her ear. "I will use it for your sake." I closed my eyes for a moment to just savour the feeling of having her alive in my arms. Then I steeled my resolve. I lifted my head.

"There is something I need you to do," I told Xinsutgen. I kissed my heart's forehead and laid her down on the ground gently. "I want you to seal her memories of the last two months."

Xinsutgen ran a hand down his face, looking aged and exhausted. He exhaled. "That will be hard; she is a Great White Mage."

I nodded. "I know, but that is alright. Once she regains her full powers, she will regain her memory as well. I just want her to enjoy life as her reincarnate, no matter how short. I want to give her the world." I gazed gently upon her beautiful face. "Or at least, the best of both her worlds."

Xinsutgen mulled it over. "Alright," he said finally. "We can try, at least. I will need your circle's magic, and we should do it at her old house."

Henceforth, her memories were sealed. The spell had worked better than we'd thought, proving once again that she was willing to give up anything for us. It would never have worked so well if she hadn't been so weak. We lifted our spells that hid the traces of our essences, and distorted the memories of all the humans who crossed paths with her. Now she would be the young girl she had secretly wanted to be.

A rueful smile found its way onto my face. She had always had too much on her mind, forgetting that I could hear her thoughts loud and clear. The times I overheard her outweighed the times she blocked me out by a wide margin. I granted her her small wish to be reunited with her parents one last time. She would fully regain her powers in about a month. In that time, she would slowly remember everything again.

We stepped into my jeep. I look out the windscreen for a moment, watching the sunrise. I recalled the time we were standing at the balcony and watched the dawn rays touch us. She had looked so beautiful then.

I started up the jeep and turned out of the hospital car park. We had a long way ahead of us.

I'll wait for you forever, I told her in my mind. I felt her surprise when she heard it. To my alarm, her heart faltered for a moment. I was pacified when the memories failed their attempt to break through to her conscious mind.

But that was alright, because she was Crescentia. We will meet again, and we will live together forever, with our circle of friends. Ezra who was sitting beside me relaxed into his seat and closed his eyes.

"So . . . what now?" he asked. He was asking all of us. Just then, Gwenwyn's traitorous stomach grumbled loudly. She blushed and giggled. I rolled my shoulders to relax into my seat as well, smiling slightly.

"So now . . . food," I said, and they laughed. I saw Quinteth jokingly nudge Gwenwyn with her elbow in the rearview mirror.

"Soon you'll be Kensington's burden," Ezra joked at Gwenwyn and she blushed right up to her roots. She stuck out her tongue at him.

"And you'll be Quinteth's burden," she retorted. The little tensions between Quinteth and Ezra had not been lost on us. I smiled in amusement as Ezra cleared his throat and looked out the window in embarrassment and it was Quinteth's turn to blush red to her roots.

I tuned out to their bickering as I usually did, and as I turned out into the highway, I left my heart behind me. As the void of loneliness filled my chest, I consoled myself with the knowledge that the girl who meant everything to me will bring it back to me, with her dazzling smile on her face.

Acknowledgements

First and foremost, I would like to offer my everlasting gratitude to my friend Alyssa Ung Sze Min, for always being more enthusiastic about my books than I am. Your feedback and honesty really helped me through.

Next, I would like to thank my parents, Liew and Marguerita, for putting up with my insanity as I rolled all over the floor for inspiration. Literally. I'd like to thank my brother, Kevin, for providing the personality for Bethamzar. You gave me good material for my antagonist. Hehe. I'd also like to thank my sister, Vanessa, for absolutely nothing. You've been no help at all. (No kidding.)

Furthermore, I want to thank my godparents, Marie and Harry, for supporting me financially and worrying about me emotionally. Sorry for being such an insane goddaughter!! Then, I want to offer my eternal and everlasting gratitude (getting melodramatic here) to my best friend, Rahula Loh and her parents, Elizabeth and Mark Jones, for always helping me in pretty much everything over the past ten years and never asking for anything in return. You guys are more valuable than gems to me. God bless ☺

I would like to thank May, my publishing consultant, for bearing with me and remaining enthusiastic about my book. This book also pays tribute to Hansel and Gretel the witch hunters. I only watched the show after completing this book and amazingly, there were loads of things in common. There's, like, a few billion more people I want to thank, so thank you everyone who has ever helped me in anything, especially this book.